THE RICH MAN'S BRIDE

BY
CATHERINE GEORGE

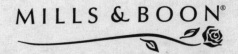

First published in Great Britain 2007
Harlequin Mills & Boon Limited,
Eton House, 18-24 Paradise Road, Richmond, Surrey TW9 1SR

© Catherine George 2007

ISBN-13: 978 0 263 85312 4
ISBN-10:   0 263 85312 8

Set in Times Roman 10 on 11½ pt
01-0407-58028

Printed and bound in Spain
by Litografia Rosés, S.A., Barcelona

He sat very still, his face a handsome mask. 'You'd actually take off now and forget any of this happened between us?'

'No, Ryder,' she said in desperation. 'I just want things to go on as they are.'

Ryder got up with such sudden violence Anna backed away. She bit her lip, shaken, and Ryder kissed her, sliding his tongue over her bottom lip. He cradled her against him, the kiss progressing from gentle to incendiary so quickly they were soon on fire, her hands as importunate as his as they kissed and caressed each other into a state of desperation.

'You see?' he said hoarsely at last. 'Admit it, Anna. You want me just as much as I want you.'

Cat... ...orge ...s born in ... developed ... passic... for reading ... ... fuelled he... compulsion to write. Marriage to an engineer led to nine years in Brazil, but on his later travels the education of her son and daughter kept her in the UK. Instead of constant reading to pass her lonely evenings, she began to write the first of her romantic novels. When not writing and reading she loves to cook, listen to opera and browse in antiques shops.

Recent titles by the same author:

AN ITALIAN ENGAGEMENT
THE MILLIONAIRE'S RUNAWAY BRIDE

THE RICH MAN'S BRIDE

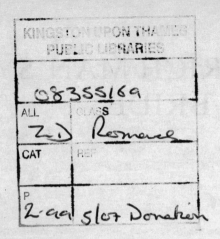

CHAPTER ONE

COLD, tired and desperate for an early night, for once Anna was glad she had the flat to herself when she got home. She gave a sigh of frustration as the bell on the street door rang and snatched up the receiver. If this was Sean, he was out of luck.

'Ryder Wyndham,' said a voice over the intercom.

Anna's eyes lit up. '*Ryder?* What a lovely surprise. Come on up.' She buzzed him in and opened her door to wait for him. She felt a sharp pang of sympathy when the new heir to the Wyndham Estate emerged from the lift. It was only months since she'd last seen him, but with his thick black curls cut close to his haggard face he looked years older and even taller than usual in a long dark overcoat over a formal suit and black tie.

She smiled warmly. 'Hi. Come in.'

Her visitor stalked past her, looking round him at the room which reflected her landlady's eclectic taste. 'Are you alone, Anna?'

No smile, not even a hello? 'Yes. How are you, Ryder?'

'I've been better.'

She nodded gravely. 'I was desperately sorry to hear about your brother. Edward's death must have been a huge shock.'

'It was,' he agreed curtly.

'Can I offer you a drink?'

He refused, giving her a head to toe scrutiny which rang warning bells in her head. 'I suppose I can see his point,' he said at last, mystifying her.

'Whose point?'

'I'm coming to that.' His eyes remained hostile. 'You don't look it, but by my calculations you must be at least thirty-three now.'

She frowned. 'You've come here to talk about my age, Ryder?'

'No, dammit,' he snarled. 'I came to tell you, face to face, to leave my brother alone.'

Anna stared at him in blank amazement. 'Dominic?'

'Who else? Eddy's dead,' he said brutally.

She took in a deep, calming breath, trying to make allowances for him. 'Look, Ryder, you're obviously under great strain. Take your coat off; let me make you a drink.'

'I don't want a drink. I want to know what the hell you're playing at!'

Anna's chin lifted. 'I think you'd better explain.'

'By all means.' His hostile eyes locked on hers. 'After Dominic came here to break the news about Eddy, you were all he could talk about—how sexy and gorgeous you are these days, and how sweet you were to him. He came up to London several times before he went back to New York—'

'You think he came to see me?' she said in disbelief.

'Officially he was visiting friends, but it's obvious now that he was coming here to visit you, Anna. I was too taken up with my various problems to suspect where it was actually leading.' His mouth twisted in disgust. 'He's barely twenty-three, so it's glaringly obvious why a woman of your age should want to marry a man so much her junior.'

'Great sex?' retorted Anna, suddenly so furious she could have hit him.

'In this case, money,' he snapped, looking down his nose in disdain. 'When Dominic told you he inherited a nice little packet from my aunt, you obviously sent the current man in your life packing and seized your chance.'

A surge of hurt anger welled up so violently it threatened to choke her. 'I can't believe you said that,' she said at last, when she could trust her voice. 'I had no idea Dominic had come into money. Nor do I care a toss if he did,' she added savagely. 'I have no intention of marrying your baby brother.'

'You expect me to believe that?' he demanded.

She stood with arms hugged across her chest. 'Whether you believe it or not, it's the truth, *Squire*. When he came to tell me about Edward it was the first time I'd seen Dominic in years. Just for the record,' she added cuttingly, 'he also paid me a second visit to say goodbye. And, if we're still counting, I caught a brief glimpse of him at the funeral.'

Ryder frowned. 'You were there? I didn't see you.'

'I left straight after the service to drive back to London.'

'I see. Your grandfather passed on your condolences, but I didn't know you'd actually made it to the church.' His eyes hardened. 'The fact remains that Dominic rang me from New York early this morning to say that you'd agreed to marry him.'

She stared in disbelief. 'If he did, he was lying—or joking. The phone's on the desk over there. Ring him right now and ask him. I won't even charge you for the call.'

Ryder shook his head. 'I've already tried, but I had no luck at his apartment and his mobile's switched off. Before we got cut off he said something about ringing me with the details tonight. I had to come up to London today to sort out probate—'

'So you came to warn me off at the same time. Or maybe even buy me off?' She gave him a taunting smile. 'What's the going rate to get shot of unsuitable brides like me, Ryder?'

He gave her an icy stare. 'That was never my intention, and you well know it.'

'Oh, I *see*!' Anna shook her head in mocking reproof. 'You expected to order me off and I'd meekly agree, with no expense involved. A bit cheap for a man with your kind of money, Ryder!'

To her intense satisfaction his eyes blazed with outrage for an instant. 'If I'm mistaken I shall, of course, apologise,' he said stiffly.

'*If?*' Her eyes flashed coldly. 'Not good enough, Squire. I demand an unqualified apology right now.'

He shook his head. 'Not until I hear from Dominic. And for God's sake stop this blasted Squire nonsense!'

'Certainly.' Anna turned on her heel, stalked to the outer door and flung it open. 'I'd like you to leave now.'

A flicker of doubt lit the dark-ringed blue eyes as Ryder passed her. 'Anna, if I'm wrong—'

'Of course you're wrong. Totally,' she said scornfully. 'And I deeply resent the insult about money. We don't see each other so much any more, but I thought you knew me better than that.'

'That's the point. So did I.' He went out on to the landing, then turned to look at her. 'Anna—'

But Anna could take no more. She slammed the door shut so he wouldn't see the tears she'd been too proud to shed in front of the new Squire of the Wyndham Estate.

Later that night Ryder Wyndham learned that his young brother's proposal of marriage had been accepted by Hannah Breckenridge, granddaughter of the founder of the New York auction house which employed him. Not by Anna Morton, granddaughter of the Wyndham Estate head gamekeeper who'd taught Dominic to shoot and fish. Appalled, Ryder rang Anna immediately to apologise. She cut him off mid-sentence and refused to pick up when he rang back. Next day he sent flowers which Anna promptly gave to the caretaker for his wife. Finally Ryder called at the flat again to apologise in person, but Anna refused to let him in, and made it bitingly clear that the ban was permanent.

When they met again, almost a year later, it was in the last place either would have wished.

The fog thickened with every mile on the road through the Marches. When a break in the swirling mist revealed the signpost she was looking for, Anna turned off to drive at a snail's pace through the familiar maze of intersecting roads and sighed with relief when she saw lights in Keeper's Cottage. She drew up in the lane behind the car parked at the gate and got out, smiling guiltily as her father hurried down the path to greet her.

'Hi, Dr Morton. They passed my message on at the surgery, then.'

'By the time I got it you were well on your way so I didn't risk ringing back.' His voice was gruff with anxiety as he gave her a hug. 'What in heaven's name possessed you to drive from London alone so soon, Anna? And in this weather!'

'Clare intended coming with me, but she started sneezing yesterday and stayed the night with her ex to avoid giving me her germs.'

'Sensible girl, your landlady,' he approved, taking her suitcase. 'I've turned the heating up to maximum, so come in quickly and get warm. If I'd known you were so determined to come, I would have fetched you.'

'Which is precisely why I didn't tell you, Dad. You lead a busy enough life as it is without flogging up to London and back for the umpteenth time again,' she said as he hurried her inside. 'I wanted to save a hard-worked doctor the trouble.'

'*I* am not recovering from pneumonia! And you look like a ghost.' Her father took her pulse, then went into the kitchen to switch on the kettle. 'I called at the village shop for eggs and milk and so on for your breakfast and the kitchen cupboards are still stocked with Father's staples. But I'll drive you to the Red Lion for dinner as soon as you've unpacked and Tom can bring you back afterwards. He should be there soon.'

Anna gave him a coaxing smile as he spooned tea-leaves into a warmed pot. 'Dad, please don't be hurt, but I'm too tired for that tonight. I promise I'll eat supper, but after that I'm off to bed. Otherwise I won't be up to much tomorrow. Apologise to my big brother.'

John Morton looked ready to argue, but in the end he nodded reluctantly and patted her cheek. 'All right, pet. An early night is probably a better idea for you. But promise me you'll eat first.'

Anna held up her hand. 'I do solemnly swear that I shall scramble some eggs. And then I'll have a bath and go to bed with a book. What time is the service tomorrow?'

'Twelve noon, then back to the Red Lion afterwards. Father's idea. He gave me his funeral instructions a while ago, complete with choice of hymns.' John cleared his throat. 'To save me any bother when the time came, he told me.'

'Oh, Dad,' whispered Anna, her eyes filling. Her father held her tightly for a moment, then took her suitcase up to her room.

'I'm really not happy about leaving you alone here tonight, Anna,' he said forcibly when he came down. 'If I'd known you meant to come, Tom and I could have stayed here with you. We still could, for that matter.'

She smiled ruefully. 'Dad, don't be offended, but just this once I really need to be on my own here.'

He touched a hand to her cheek. 'I understand. Now, I'd better go. But, for God's sake, ring if you feel ill.'

'Dad, I'll be fine!'

'I hope so.' He kissed her cheek. 'I'll be round in the morning early to make sure you've had breakfast.'

Anna waved him off, then suddenly so weary she needed to hang on to the rope looped through rings fastened in the wall she went upstairs. When she made it to the top she leaned in the open doorway of her grandfather's room for a moment to catch her breath. Formal photographs of herself and Tom at their degree ceremonies stood on the chest of drawers, alongside a small snapshot of them with Ryder Wyndham, all three youngsters grinning in triumph as they held up the trout they'd caught. She gazed at it through a mist of tears, then scrubbed at her eyes, blew her nose and went next door to her own room to unpack a black suit she normally wore to work. Black was no longer mandatory for funerals these days, but her grandfather would have expected his family to show proper respect. And no one deserved it more than Hector Morton.

In the bathroom later Anna's eyebrows rose in surprise. The expensive fittings and gleaming white paint were all new since her last visit. Her mouth tightened as she went downstairs. The squire certainly believed in keeping up the value on his property.

Just a few months previously the small kitchen had been fitted with new cupboards and appliances and the overpowering black of the overhead beams shot-blasted back to the original wood throughout the house to add light. And it still amazed her that so much trouble had been taken over a tied cottage. Hector Morton had once been head gamekeeper of the estate, it was true. His original home had been a sizeable house which went with the job, but after his wife died he'd requested a move to Keeper's Cottage, which Anna fell in love with at the age of eight because it looked like something from Hansel and Gretel. The exterior's wreathing wisteria and latticed windows still retained the fairy-tale look, but since the renovations the interior looked like something from a magazine.

Anna went to the pantry to fetch eggs for her supper and discovered that part of the room had been partitioned off to create a brand-new shower cubicle. She began to laugh and ran to the parlour, fully expecting to find the giant inglenook fireplace transformed into a conservatory at the very least. But here all was more or less familiar. The two sofas had new fawn slip covers but they still faced each other in front of the big fireplace, with the familiar little Jacobean table in its place between them, and four Windsor chairs were still grouped with a small folding dining table against the inner wall. The shock discovery here was a brand-new television.

Anna rang her father before starting on her supper. 'What on earth has been going on here, Dad?'

'I thought you'd enjoy the surprise,' John said, chuckling. 'The bathroom had a makeover when the shower went in downstairs, but I'm to blame for the television. I bought it when Father had that bout of flu and couldn't go out—though I doubt that he ever watched anything other than newscasts.'

'I doubt it, too! Love to Tom. I'll see you both in the morning.'

After supper Anna had a quick bath, then pulled on pyjamas and fleece dressing gown and went to work on her hair, praying that a good night's sleep would do something for the circles under her eyes. But once she was settled against stacked pillows later she felt a lot better, as she always did the moment she was through the door of Keeper's Cottage.

True to his word, John Morton arrived at nine next morning to find his daughter at the table, reading yesterday's paper. She smiled smugly as she held her face up for his kiss.

'There!' She showed him the remains of her toast and marmalade. 'I've eaten breakfast. Have you?'

'Far too much.' He patted his spare midriff ruefully.

'What's Tom doing?'

'I told him to have a lie-in for once, but he's up now. When I left he was wolfing down everything the Red Lion had to offer.' John glanced at the paper Anna had been reading. 'I thought I'd cancelled that.'

'It's mine. I brought it with me.' She handed him a cup of tea. 'Sit down for a minute, Dad. There's something I want to say.'

His dark eyes narrowed anxiously. 'That sounds ominous!'

'Not really.' She braced herself. 'It's just that if Ryder Wyndham gives me permission I'd like to do my convalescing here at the cottage.'

Her father frowned. 'But this place is a bit isolated, Anna. Are you sure it's a good idea?'

'Yes,' she said firmly. 'I feel much better already, after just one night here.'

He eyed her closely. 'You certainly look more rested.'

'For the first time in ages I slept like a baby.' Anna looked at him in appeal. 'Dad, you and Tom both saw Gramp more recently than I did, thanks to my stay in hospital. I really need this time here to say my goodbyes to him.'

He nodded slowly in agreement. 'I'm sure an old friend like Ryder won't object.' He downed his tea and stood up. 'Right. I must get back. Several people arrived last night, but quite a few more are booked in for today, so I'd better be on hand with Tom when they turn up. I'll be back for you at—'

'No, you won't, Dad! There's no point in doubling back

from the village to collect me. I'll drive over and meet you both there.'

He shook his head. 'Stubborn to the last! We'll wait for you outside the church, then. And wear something warm.'

'Yes, Doctor.'

Anna kissed him goodbye, then cleared away the breakfast pots and went upstairs to deal with the bright hair inherited from the mother who'd died when Anna was eight. Of pneumonia, she thought with contrition. No wonder her father was concerned. But, unlike her delicate mother, she was normally as fit as a fiddle. By the time she'd vegetated here for a few days—subject to the Squire's approval, she reminded herself acidly—she'd be strong as a horse again and ready to get back to her job.

At ten-thirty she was ready in the slim black suit worn with a silk camisole over one of the lacy vests Clare had waiting when Anna was discharged from hospital. She added a long black overcoat, brushed a stray tendril back into her upswept knot of hair and put on dark glasses. She locked up carefully and then on impulse picked a posy of snowdrops from a flower bed, and threaded them through a buttonhole.

When Anna arrived at the church it was no surprise to find a long line of cars there before her. Hector Morton had been much respected as well as universally liked. A decent turnout was only to be expected. Anna smiled as her brother, sober-suited and his thatch of dark hair tidy for once, hurried to give her a rib-cracking hug as he helped her out of the car.

'You look pale but gorgeous with it,' he said, holding her away to look at her. 'I like the celebrity shades.'

'Camouflage in case I cry.' She eyed him in approval. 'You look pretty good yourself, Tom. After the long hours you moan about I thought you'd be wan and haggard.'

'I was when I got here, but the cure was simple—a night's sleep followed by the biggest breakfast of my entire life,' he informed her, grinning. 'And, unless that's a very clever paint job, you look a damn sight better than you did in hospital.'

'I'm absolutely fine now,' she said firmly as they joined their father.

John kissed her cheek. 'You look lovely, darling.' He took Anna and Tom aside as the hearse glided to a stop outside the lych-gate. 'We follow him down the aisle,' he said in an undertone.

Faced with the harsh reality of the flower-crowned coffin, Anna heaved in an unsteady breath, grateful for Tom's support-ing arm as they entered the church. From that moment on the entire service passed in one long act of self-control. She sang the hymns her grandfather had chosen and even managed to listen without breaking down when her father spoke with humour and deep affection about Hector Morton, beloved father, grandfather and lifelong friend to many of those present.

In the churchyard later Ryder Wyndham stood slightly apart from the other mourners, watching as Anna took snowdrops from her buttonhole to let them drift down on the coffin in silent goodbye. When she looked up at last she gazed at him for a moment through the dark, concealing lenses, then inclined her head in slight, unsmiling acknowledgement and turned away.

Shaken by the silent exchange, Anna would have given much to drive straight back to the cottage there and then. Instead she walked across the village green to the Red Lion and took her place beside her father and Tom to welcome an assortment of relatives and friends. She responded to kisses and condolences, assured people that she was well now and listened to affection-ate reminiscences about her grandfather. Her tension mounted steadily until at last, during one of her regular checks to make sure no elderly relative was left alone, she saw Ryder Wyndham approaching.

'How good of you to come,' she said formally and held out her hand very deliberately to prevent him from kissing her cheek, as most other people had done.

He shook the hand briefly, his handsome face grave. 'Hector was my oldest friend, Anna. I shall miss him very much.'

'So shall I.'

'Hi there, Squire,' said Tom as he came to join them. 'Long time no see.'

'Far too long, Doctor.' Ryder smiled warmly as he shook Tom's hand. 'You should take a break and go fishing with me again.'

'Nothing I'd like better,' said Tom promptly. 'Look, we're staying here tonight. Why not come over for a drink and a chat later when it's quiet?'

'Thank you. I may well do that.' Ryder turned to Anna with concern. 'You're very pale. Let me get you some brandy.'

'She's just out of hospital. This was a huge strain for her today,' said Tom, eyeing her closely. 'How do you feel, love?'

'Absolutely fine,' she assured him and smiled politely at Ryder. 'I'll pass on the brandy, thanks, but I would like a word with you. Could you spare me a few moments tomorrow at the cottage—Mr Wyndham?'

His jaw clenched at the formality. 'Of course, whatever time suits you.'

'Eleven, then?'

'Eleven it is. Now, if you'll excuse me, I must speak to your father.'

Anna nodded graciously. 'Thank you so much for coming.'

'You knew I'd be here.' He turned to smile at Tom. 'I meant it about the fishing. Give me a ring when the season starts.'

'You bet, Ryder. Thanks a lot.'

Anna watched Ryder Wyndham thread his way through the room, pausing to speak with various people as he went.

'Did I detect a certain *froideur* towards the Squire?' asked Tom dryly.

'Better not call him that to his face. I've heard he doesn't like it.'

'He wasn't too keen on the Mr Wyndham tag, either. What was all that about?'

She shrugged. 'It seemed to suit the occasion.'

'He was right, though. You look ready to drop.' Tom gave her a professional scrutiny. 'Look, I've had nothing much to drink yet, Anna. I'll drive you back to Keeper's. I can get your car back to you tomorrow.'

She shook her head firmly. 'No, thanks, Tom. I'll be much happier if you stay here to support Dad.'

Some people took so long over their leave-taking it was an hour before Anna could kiss her father goodbye and let Tom walk her to her car.

'Text me as soon as you get back,' he ordered. 'And drive carefully.'

'It's not far, Tom!'

It was exactly three miles door to door from the church to Keeper's Cottage, but it felt more like thirty to Anna by the time she parked outside in the lane. The garden path seemed longer than usual and the cottage so dark and quiet she switched on all the lights before sending a message to Tom to report in. Shivering with a mixture of reaction and cold, she turned up the heating and went upstairs to change. With a sigh of relief, she toed off her high black heels and exchanged her mourning black for grey flannel trousers, her heaviest roll-neck sweater and the sheepskin slippers her grandfather had bought for her in the local market on her last visit. She'd laughed at the time, but right now her icy, aching toes were deeply grateful for their warmth.

After a phone call to Clare to ask about her cold and report that all had gone smoothly, Anna unpinned her hair and wove it into a loose braid, then went downstairs to begin the ritual of making tea in her grandfather's brown pot. She could cry at last if she wanted. But, in the perverse way of such things, she had no tears left now there was no one to see.

While Anna was looking through the cupboards to decide on her supper menu, Tom rang to ask if she'd changed her mind about having dinner with them.

'No, Tom. The cottage is warm and, much as I'll miss your company, I'd rather stay here and open a tin.'

He sighed. 'OK, if you're sure, Anna. It just seems wrong that we're here and you're up there alone.'

'As soon as you and Dad get a weekend off together I'll cook dinner in the flat. Clare would love that. So would I.'

'Me too, great idea. OK—no more nagging. We'll call in to see you when we set off in the morning. Have a good night, but ring if you need us.'

'I'll probably sleep like a log again. This cottage has good vibes for me, Tom, always has.'

'I know. Otherwise Dad wouldn't let you stay there alone, even at your age.'

Anna smiled as she rang off. These days no one 'let' her do anything; not even her father.

The doorbell rang while she was watching the ten o'clock news. She smiled fondly. Her father hadn't been able to resist checking up on her after all. To reassure him that she was security conscious, she kept the new safety chain on as she opened the door, but her smile vanished as unmistakable blue eyes looked down at her through the aperture. The Squire, it seemed, had honoured his tenant with a visit.

'May I come in, Anna?' said Ryder Wyndham.

Her first instinct was a flat refusal for several reasons, not least because she was wearing the famous slippers and her face probably looked as grey as her sweater now her make-up had worn off. On the other hand, she needed a favour.

'I won't keep you long,' he added.

Anna unhooked the chain and opened the door. 'Come in, then.'

Her visitor followed her into the parlour, his hair, longer again now, almost brushing the beams. Anna waved him to a sofa and took the one opposite, wondering, not for the first time, if some gypsy blood had once nourished the Wyndham family tree. In his teens Ryder had traded on the look, sporting wild black ringlets and a gold earring that went well with slanting cheekbones and eyes surrounded by lashes that were still thick as flue-brushes, she thought resentfully. At the moment the eyes were surveying her with unnerving concentration.

'In the churchyard today that knot of hair shone like a beacon among all the mourning black,' he said at last, surprising her. 'But worn like that you look about fifteen.'

'Such a good thing for a woman to hear when she's more than twice that age,' said Anna, her tone as sweet and cold as the lemon sorbet she was partial to.

'I know exactly how old you are.'

Her eyes glittered coldly. 'You've told me that before.'

'I called in at the Red Lion,' Ryder said after an awkward silence. 'Tom told me you came straight back here, too tired to stay there for dinner.'

'It's been a tiring sort of day.'

'And you've been ill.'

She shrugged. 'Something I'll do my utmost to avoid in future. It worried my family and interfered with my job.'

The striking eyes remained steady on her face. 'Are you still with the same firm of chartered accountants?'

She nodded. 'Yes. I hope to make partner soon.'

'So I heard. Your grandfather was very proud of your success. He thought the world of you, Anna.'

'It was mutual.' She looked at him levelly. 'Why did you come tonight instead of in the morning?'

'Your father asked me to call in to check on you.'

She frowned impatiently. 'He really shouldn't have done that.'

'It's no great thing. I had to pass the cottage on my way home, Anna.' Ryder stood up, his presence filling the low-ceilinged room. In place of the black tie and dark suit of the afternoon he wore a heavy navy sweater with casual cords, but as always, Anna thought resentfully, looked exactly right.

'Since you are here we might as well talk now and save you some time,' she said shortly, but he shook his head.

'You look exhausted, Anna. I'll come back in the morning.

Goodnight. Sleep well.' He looked down at her as she opened the front door. 'Put the chain on after I leave.'

She gave him a curt nod. 'Goodnight.'

Anna had been tired and ready for bed before Ryder Wyndham turned up. But sleep was a forlorn hope now without a warm bath to soothe down the hackles her visitor had raised without even trying. She knew perfectly well that she should have said her piece tonight, but sheer vanity had prodded her to look more appealing when she coaxed Ryder to let her stay in the cottage for a while.

Anna groaned next morning when she faced her reflection in the bathroom mirror. Looking like this she was in no state to do any coaxing. Her hair was a wild tangle after the steam of her late night bath and her face was milk-pale—something she'd have to put right pretty sharply before her father and Tom arrived and carted her off home to Shrewsbury whether she wanted to go or not.

Later, in a scarlet sweater chosen to lend warmth to her skin, Anna did some skilful work on her face, but her efforts failed to deceive the brace of doctors she was related to.

'Bad night, obviously,' said her father, looking worried.

'My own fault. I took an unplanned nap during the evening,' she told him. 'Fortunately I was awake when Ryder called. Bad idea, Dad. You shouldn't have asked him to do that.'

John Morton eyed her in surprise. 'I knew he'd be passing on his way home. Besides, I thought you'd be pleased to see him.'

'I was not looking my best by that time,' she said tartly. 'Not that it matters. Have you two got time for coffee before you take off?'

'Sorry,' said Tom regretfully. 'I'm doing an outpatients clinic at two.'

'And I'm seeing Father's solicitor on the way back, so I must be off too,' said John Morton, and peered into his daughter's eyes as he felt her pulse. 'How soon will you finish your antibiotics?'

'Ten days to go.'

'Good. But you look a bit anaemic to me, my girl. Add some extra iron to your vitamins.'

'I'm already doing that, Dad.'

Once Anna had persuaded her men that she was perfectly capable of managing alone for a day or two, they drove off, one after the other, leaving her to wait for another visit from the Squire.

Ryder Wyndham arrived promptly at eleven, by which time Anna's hair was in a careless-looking knot that had taken ages to achieve, and both she and the cottage were immaculate.

'Good morning,' said Anna as she let him in. 'Coffee?'

'Thank you.'

She opened the parlour door for him, but he followed her to the kitchen.

'How are you today, Anna?'

'Absolutely fine. Would you take the tray?'

When they were seated opposite each other in the parlour, Ryder took the cup she gave him and sat back. 'For obvious reasons I was surprised when you asked to see me. So what can I do for you, Anna?'

She smiled politely. 'Nothing too arduous. I just need your permission to stay on in the cottage for a few days. I'm supposed to convalesce for a while before even thinking of going back to work, and I'll do that far better here than in London.'

He shrugged. 'You don't need my permission, Anna. It's your grandfather's house, not mine. He bought it from the estate years ago.'

'*What?*' She stared at him blankly. 'Is that true?'

He looked down his aquiline Wyndham nose. 'I'm not in the habit of lying, Anna. I admit it's not our normal policy to sell off property, but Hector Morton served the estate faithfully all his working life, so my father made an exception in his case.'

Anna shook her head in amazement. 'I had no idea.'

'Surely you wondered why so much work was done here this past year?'

'I assumed the Wyndham Estate was responsible.'

He shook his head. 'My total input was to give any advice your grandfather asked for.'

'It was very good advice, Ryder,' she conceded. 'The entire cottage looks a picture. Though I'm surprised he bothered at his age. He knew very well he wouldn't have long to enjoy it,' she added sadly.

'His own enjoyment was never his intention. He was making the place more saleable.'

'He meant to *sell* it?' she said, startled.

'No.' Ryder put his cup on the tray and got up. 'Anna, this puts me in a very awkward position. Hector showed me his will quite recently, but you obviously know nothing about it.'

'Not yet. Dad's calling in on the solicitor on his way back this morning. He'll ring me tonight.'

'Good. He can put you in the picture. How long will you stay here?' he added.

'A few days, maybe. I'll see how it goes.' Anna got to her feet, eyeing him in challenge. 'Do you *mind* if I stay for a while, Ryder?'

'Of course not.' He smiled bleakly. 'After all, we were good friends once.'

'Something you forgot one memorable evening,' she said bluntly.

'Anna, if I could take back the things I said that night I would. It was a pretty rough time for me. I apologised humbly when I knew the truth,' he reminded her curtly.

Anna eyed him with scorn. 'Come off it, Ryder. You don't do humble.'

His eyes glittered coldly. 'I had a damn good try in your case! I failed spectacularly, I grant you, but your grandfather told me to give you time, that you'd come round one day.'

'Did he really? For once in his life he was wrong.'

He gave her a challenging look. 'Was he? In London you

wouldn't let me through the door, but here you've done that twice in two days.'

'Only because I needed something from you,' she assured him. 'Have you heard from Dominic lately?'

'Yes. I told him about Hector. I wouldn't pass on the number here without your permission so Dominic asked me to give you his condolences.'

'If he contacts you again, give him the number by all means, but I doubt that he'll need it.'

'You're not so friendly with my little brother these days?'

Her eyes clashed with his. 'I never was in the way you mean. In any case Dominic lives in New York now—and soon he'll be married to someone much younger and a lot more eligible than me,' she added tartly. 'Tell me, Ryder. Was it just my advancing years you objected to, or the irrefutable fact that I was your gamekeeper's granddaughter?'

His face hardened. 'That's an insult to your grandfather.'

'Then I apologise to him. Thank you so much for coming,' she added graciously. 'I'm sorry I wasted your valuable time.'

'Not at all.' He shook her hand with cold formality. 'If you have any problems, don't hesitate to get in touch.'

She'd crawl over hot coals first!

At the front door he paused to look down at her. 'Take good care of yourself, Anna. Tom told me you developed pneumonia because you went back to work too soon after a dose of flu.'

Her eyes flashed. 'Tom should mind his own business!'

'As a brother and a doctor,' he drawled, 'I imagine he feels that your health *is* his business.'

'True, but it's very definitely not yours, Ryder Wyndham— or should I say Squire and pull my forelock?'

'By all means if you want to, Anna,' he said, infuriating her, and fixed her with a glacial blue look. 'Tom told me you'd been ill for the simple reason that he wanted me to keep an eye on you. Here's my mobile number. Call me if you need anything.'

'How kind. But I won't,' she assured him, and held the door open wide.

'Keep the card anyway.' Ryder nodded casually and went down the path to the Land Rover waiting at the gate.

CHAPTER TWO

ANNA heard from her father before he began evening surgery. 'What's up, Dad?' she said, surprised. 'I thought you were ringing tonight.'

'I just couldn't wait that long to give you my news, darling—'

'Hold on. Before you start, I've got news for you too. Ryder says Gramp bought the cottage from the estate years ago. Did you know about that?'

'No—at least not until this morning. Father left the cottage to you, Anna.'

She sat down with a thump on one of the kitchen chairs. *'What?'*

'You get the cottage, and he put a sum of money equal to its value in trust for Tom and me. Old Fanshawe's a dry old stick, but he had a twinkle in his eye when he told me my father had been playing the stock market for years. The old devil. He let me assume that the estate was paying for the work on the cottage. And all the time he was turning it into a desirable property to leave to you. He made it over to you years ago, Anna. Are you still there?'

'Just about,' she said faintly.

'I'm having trouble taking it in too,' admitted John Morton. 'I had no idea Father had so much money to leave. But I wish he'd left it differently, instead of landing you with the responsibility of the house.'

'Knowing Gramp, he had his reasons, Dad.'

'He obviously expected you to sell it.'

Anna looked round her with assessing eyes. 'I'm not so sure about that. He knew how much I loved the place, so maybe he thought I'd live here.'

'You can't commute to London, Anna!'

'True. But it would be a perfect weekend retreat for all three of us.'

'That hardly seems fair.'

'What does Tom say about it?'

'I haven't told him yet.' John Morton's voice softened. 'Now, forget about the will for a minute—how do you feel, darling?'

'Thunderstruck.'

'I mean physically.'

Anna thought about it. 'Is a sudden yearning for bacon sandwiches a good sign?'

'Excellent. But I didn't buy any bacon for you.'

'It's a fine afternoon. I'll drive down to the village shop.'

'Good idea. Buy plenty of milk and fresh fruit too. Take care of yourself, pet. I'll ring you tomorrow.'

Anna put on the ancient sheepskin jacket always kept in her wardrobe at Keeper's and went out to the car, delighted by the idea of her grandfather playing the stock market. Good for him, she thought proudly as she drove through cold late afternoon sunshine.

Anna left the village stores later with a bag full of shopping and a head buzzing with condolences and local news, but arrived home with a proud sense of achievement because she'd managed it all without feeling exhausted. Her *own* home, she reminded herself in triumph. Keeper's Cottage was now officially her very own property, all signed and sealed. She couldn't wait to tell Clare.

Clare Saunders was an attractive forty-year-old divorcee, who owned a flat bought with her share of the proceeds when her marriage to a fellow journalist came to an end. The two women had met at a party and took to each other on sight—so much so that when Clare heard Anna was in sudden need for

somewhere to live she suggested they try sharing for a month to
see how it worked out. It worked out so well that John and Tom
Morton soon looked on Clare as an extra member of the family.

With no chance of talking to her friend until Clare got home
from work that evening, Anna settled down with a book for the
daily rest her father had insisted on as part of her recovery pro-
gramme. But excitement over her windfall made it hard to rest
and even harder to concentrate on the written word. Her mouth
tightened. A shame she hadn't known all this sooner. There
would have been no need to coax Ryder Wyndham to let her stay
here. Though at one time that would have posed no problem at
all. As he'd reminded her, they'd been good friends when they
were young.

She gave up on her book and leaned back, her mind on the
past. She'd spent almost every school holiday here with Tom
after their mother died. Hector Morton had been only too pleased
to look after his grandchildren, ready to give any help he could
to his grieving, hard-working doctor son. He'd kept a watchful,
tolerant eye on Anna and Tom as they roamed the estate with
Ryder. Edward Wyndham, the eldest son, was several years
Ryder's senior and, as heir to the estate, too involved in helping
his father run it to have time for siblings. Dominic had surprised
everyone, not least his parents, by appearing on the scene when
Ryder was thirteen and Anna ten.

But five years after that everything changed for Anna.

The Wyndhams gave a party to celebrate Ryder's eighteenth
birthday and, to her wild excitement, Anna received a formal
invitation. John Morton bought her the dress of her dreams and
Hector drove her to the Manor that night, proud as Punch of
his granddaughter. Anna received a warm welcome from all the
family, but felt shy as she was introduced to the other guests.
The boys were friendly, but the girls ignored her. They were
sophisticated creatures, with long hair and strapless satin
dresses, and the moment she laid eyes on them Anna found that
her new elfin haircut and pastel chiffon party frock were all

wrong. For the first time in her life she was conscious of the social gulf which yawned between Anna Morton from Keeper's Cottage and Ryder Wyndham from the Manor. His mother, unfailingly kind as always, made sure that her youngest guest never lacked for partners when the disco music started thumping out in the marquee, but once supper was over Anna couldn't get away fast enough. She thanked her hostess and, with the excuse that her grandfather was waiting for her, slipped away, desperate to go home.

But Ryder went racing after her and when he found that Hector's old shooting brake was nowhere in sight, drove her home in the sports car he'd been given for his birthday. He'd laughingly demanded a goodnight kiss for taxi fare, the first they'd ever exchanged, and with a careless wave drove back to the party, leaving Anna to stand at the gate gazing after him in a daze. To Ryder the kiss had so obviously meant nothing more than an affectionate exchange with an old friend that Anna suffered a crushing sense of rejection as he returned at top speed to the Manor, eager to get back to the girls who'd been so hostile towards her. Anna watched the scarlet car roar away into the night and knew that nothing would be the same again. It was time to grow up.

Life also changed for the youngest Wyndham. According to Hector, Dominic grew up wild and rebellious, narrowly missed being expelled from school after his mother died, and insisted on taking a fine art course instead of studying law as his father wanted. Anna hadn't seen him for years until the evening he came to tell her about Edward Wyndham's sudden, tragic death.

She had been dressed ready for a party and knew with hindsight that she'd made more of an impression on her visitor than she'd realised in a clinging black sheath with her hair in an expensively tousled amber mane. But, no matter what Dominic said to his brother afterwards, she thought bitterly, she had merely offered her visitor coffee and sympathy, and even offered a tissue when his feelings overcame him and tears welled in the familiar blue Wyndham eyes. They had talked over old times together, and Dominic described his job in the fine arts section of a prestigious New York auction house, of the 'nose' he'd developed for finding sleepers that turned out to be lost masterpieces. He'd also talked a lot about the wonderful girl he worked with there. When Anna asked after Ryder, Dominic told her his brother was keeping his feelings under wraps, as usual. But Anna had eventually learnt exactly how Ryder felt the night he came to confront her with his accusations. And, even after all this time, the wound he'd inflicted was still painful.

Anna shrugged the memories away as she made supper. Afterwards she rang Clare to pass on the astonishing news about her legacy and tried to coax her friend to come down for the weekend. But Clare was now deep in the throes of her cold and in no state to go anywhere but bed.

'Sorry, can't make it, love,' she said thickly. 'It's a good thing you're safe out of the way down there. The last thing you need is assault and battery by a new set of germs.'

'You sound terrible, Clare. For heaven's sake look after yourself—remember what happened to me!'

'A salutary lesson, darling. Never fear, I'm dosing myself with pills washed down with hot lemon and honey laced with single malt my dear old ex brought me.'

'Is Charlie with you?'

'He's mopping my feverish brow as we speak.'

Anna grinned as she heard familiar male laughter. 'I'll leave you to enjoy ill health, then. Take care.'

Tom rang later to exclaim over their grandfather's legacy. 'Will you sell the cottage, Anna?'

'It's the sensible thing to do, but I don't want to. As I told Dad, the three of us can use it as a weekend retreat.'

'But that's not fair. You didn't get any cash, and you'll need some just to keep the place ticking over.'

'I know that, Tom, but I can manage that quite easily on my

salary. Besides, this place is so full of Gramp I can't bear the thought of strangers living here.'

'Me too, but you may well change your mind after a few days on your own down there.'

CHAPTER THREE

DETERMINED to prove Tom wrong, Anna settled into a pleasant, restful routine. She slept reasonably well, drove to the village after breakfast every morning for a daily paper and anything else she fancied, then after lunch went for a walk if the weather was good or a drive when it rained. By the evening she was only too happy to talk on the phone with friends for a while before settling on a sofa with a book, or to watch television, and her mirror confirmed that she looked a lot better. To her relief she saw no more of Ryder Wyndham, but her father checked on her daily and promised to drive down to take her to lunch at the Red Lion the following Saturday.

Anna spent the morning tidying up the day before, went for a drive in the afternoon and on the way back called in at the village shop to lay in extra supplies for her father's visit. She was so late getting back it was dark by the time she reached the cottage. She dumped her shopping down in the hall and switched on lights, then went into the parlour to draw the curtains. And stopped dead in the doorway. The place was a mess. The sofa cushions had been thrown to the floor and the television was missing, along with two oil paintings and the set of Spode plates from the inglenook… She stiffened, swallowing dryly. The intruder could still be in the house. Armed with a poker from the fireplace, she tiptoed through to the pantry but, to her enormous relief, met no one on the way. The burglar was long gone, taking the microwave, kettle and kitchen wall clock with him, she noted in fury. A chill ran down her spine. He might be upstairs.

Anna forced herself to creep up the narrow staircase, then sagged against the wall on the landing in relief when she found no sign of the intruder other than the chaos he'd caused. She stayed on the landing to look into each bedroom and ground her teeth in fury at the sight of drawers yanked out of the furniture and mattresses heaved to one side. As the final straw, her suitcase had been opened and her underwear tossed in a tangled heap on the carpet. But she was wearing her watch and signet ring and she'd taken her wallet with her, so the pickings in that field had been slim for the intruder, which was some consolation. Her instinct was to rush into each room and tidy up, but caution told her to leave everything as it was and ring the police to report the break-in. After making the call she found she was trembling with reaction. She knew she ought to ring her father. But he was a long way away and well into evening surgery by now and Tom had even further to drive, even if he was available.

Nevertheless she was in urgent need of support from someone right now. In the end she searched for Ryder's card, stared at it for a long moment, then shrugged and rang his number. Hot coals or not, this was an emergency.

'Ryder, it's Anna. I'm sorry to trouble you, but I didn't know who else to ring. I've been burgled.'

'Good God. Are you all right? Are you hurt?' he demanded.

'No. I was out. I've just got in. I've rung the police.'

'Good. I'm on my way.'

Anna put her shopping away while she waited, but in shorter time than she'd have believed possible she heard a car speeding down the lane, footsteps racing up the path and hammering on the door.

'Anna, let me in.'

She threw open the door and Ryder closed it behind him, his face stern.

'Tell me what happened,' he ordered.

'I went out this afternoon,' she said unsteadily. 'When I came back I found the place in a mess and some things had been taken. My first thought was to ring Dad, but it would have taken him ages to get here and you did say to contact you if I needed anything.'

'Of course. It was exactly the right thing to do,' he said, eyeing her closely. 'Are you sure you're all right, Anna? You're as white as a sheet.'

'Fright,' she said tersely. 'I'm fine otherwise.'

'Good. Come and sit down and tell me what's missing.' His voice was so sympathetic Anna fought an urge to lay her head on his shoulder and cry her eyes out. 'Hector's obituary was in the local paper today,' he said grimly. 'Someone obviously read it and came to take a look.'

She stared at him, aghast. 'You think it was as calculated as that?'

'It's pretty common practice. What was taken?'

Anna ticked off the list on her fingers as she told him. 'Luckily Gramp gave me Grandma's jewellery ages ago…' She bit her lip.

'What is it?'

'I've just remembered. Gramp had a gold watch—a half hunter with a heavy gold chain and fob. I didn't look, but they probably got away with that as well.' She gave a shiver. 'They ransacked the drawers and threw some of my things on the floor, but I didn't actually go in the bedrooms. I left that for the police.'

'Good thinking,' approved Ryder. 'You look shaken, Anna. I'll make you some tea while we wait for them.'

'You don't have to wait.'

'Don't talk rot,' he said brusquely.

Anna groaned in dismay. 'You can't make tea. They've taken the kettle.'

'What a townie you are these days,' he mocked. 'A saucepan on the stove will do the job just as well—provided they left the tea.'

'It should be in the caddy with the portrait of the Queen.'

'I know. Hector often made tea for me in that big brown pot,' said Ryder soberly. 'I miss him too, Anna—' He broke off as the bell rang and went to the door to let in the police.

The constables who came in answer to Anna's call had known Hector Morton well. They offered condolences, made a thorough inspection and found the window broken in the spare bedroom. The burglar had climbed up the wisteria, smashed the glass next to the window latch and hopped over the window sill, splintering wood and tearing curtains down in the process as he rushed to let his partner in through the front door. Ryder assured the policemen that he'd block up the window until a glazier could be organised and, after providing the men with a list of everything she knew to be missing, Anna felt weary by the time they left.

'I don't care about the television and the electrical stuff they took,' she told Ryder as he finally gave her the promised tea, 'but the paintings and plates and the kitchen clock were Gramp's wedding presents.'

'It won't be easy to track them down, Anna. There are so many cop shows on television every likely lad wears gloves to do his breaking and entering these days,' he pointed out.

She nodded, depressed. 'Dad's coming to take me to lunch tomorrow. When I tell him about this he'll insist on taking me home with him. In the meantime I'd better ring the Red Lion—'

'Why?'

She pulled a face. 'I don't fancy sleeping here tonight with a broken window for company.'

'You're not going to. You're coming home with me.'

Anna stared at him in surprise. 'I can't do that.'

'Why not?'

She could think of a great many reasons, none of which she wanted to share with Ryder.

'I'm not exactly short of bedrooms,' he reminded her. 'And Mrs Carter is still around. God knows what I'll do when she retires. She's been a godsend since I took over. I employ plenty of help from the village, but she's getting on a bit and does so much I tend to worry about her.'

'Is staff easy to find?'

'The women who help in the house have been working there for years, so up to now the problem hasn't arisen. The estate manager retired recently and I haven't found anyone to take over his job yet so I'm doing that myself as a learning exercise. My father and Eddy died within months of each other, which meant double death duties, so there's a lot to sort out.'

'So Dominic told me.'

Ryder smiled sardonically. 'Did he mention that my engagement ended about that time as well?'

'No, he didn't. Tom told me only recently. I'm sorry,' she added awkwardly.

He shrugged. 'Past history now. Right then, Anna, if you can supply me with a plastic bag I'll raid Hector's tool box for some masking tape and seal that window while you pack some things for the night.'

Not, thought Anna as she handed him a bin liner, that she was as sorry as she should be about the missing fiancée. Edwina French had been one of the unfriendly girls at the party all those years ago.

Ryder made short work of sealing the bedroom window, made a note of the splintered ledge and crumbling plaster the burglar had left in his wake, and went along the landing to Anna's room. He frowned when he saw the tangle of underwear on her floor. 'You can't wear any of that!'

'Absolutely not,' she said, shuddering, and stepped over it to look in her wardrobe. 'Nothing seems to be touched in here, thank goodness. My sweaters are still in their polythene bags. I'll just throw the other things in the bath—'

'Stuff them in a bag instead and take them with you. Mrs Carter will run them through the washing machine and have them ready by morning.'

'The poor woman has enough to do without that. I'll ask her to let me do it,' said Anna firmly.

'You can ask, but she'll take one look at you and rush you off to bed.'

Ryder was right. He rang Mrs Carter to tell her he was bringing Anna to stay the night, and why, and by the time they arrived she had prepared a room and had the kitchen door open the moment Ryder drove into the back courtyard. Neat as always in a navy dress and flowered apron, every grey hair in place, she beamed in welcome as Ryder helped Anna down from the Land Rover.

Unlike the black and white half-timbered houses common to most local architecture, the Manor was a classic Georgian cube with a pillared portico and floor to ceiling windows. Anna glanced up at them with a shiver, remembering the light blazing from them as she made her escape from Ryder's party all those years ago.

'Here she is, Martha,' said Ryder.

'You poor dear,' said the housekeeper as Ryder took Anna inside. 'What a thing to happen.'

'I'm sorry to give you so much trouble, Mrs Carter,' said Anna. 'Ryder said you wouldn't mind if I put some things in your washing machine. The intruder pawed through them and left them in a heap on the floor.'

'Dirty beast,' said Mrs Carter fiercely. 'Just you hand them over, dear. I'll see to them. I've put you in the little blue guest room because it heats up the quickest, but I've put hot-water bottles in the bed just in case. I'll bring you a tray of supper after you've had a rest.'

Maternal coddling had been missing from Anna's life since she was eight and, after the shock of the robbery, it was the last straw for her self-control. 'So sorry,' she said thickly, mopping at tears.

'Don't you apologise. You've got every right to cry after such a nasty shock. Now, I'll see to these things while Mr Ryder takes you up to your room.'

Anna blew her nose and followed Ryder up a panelled stair-case lined with portraits of former Wyndhams. He took her along the landing to a small, reassuringly cosy guest room, eyeing her searchingly as he put her bag down. 'Do you really want to go straight to bed?'

She shook her head. 'Are you going out?' she asked awkwardly.

'No.'

'Then could I just sit downstairs with you?'

'Of course,' he said courteously. 'If that's what you prefer, I'd be delighted to have your company, Anna. I'll tell Martha. Your bathroom's through that blue door. In the meantime, take it easy for a while. I'll be back for you in an hour.'

Anna felt grubby from mere contact with the clothes the intruder had handled. She would have liked a bath, but with no clean underwear at her disposal she contented herself with a vigorous wash before changing into the red sweater she'd packed. When Ryder came back for her she was sitting in a small blue armchair by the window, leafing through out-of-date magazines.

'You look much better,' he said in approval, then smiled as he noticed her reading matter. 'We used to provide those for guests, but I haven't done much entertaining since my father and Eddy died.'

'Because you're still grieving for them, Ryder?' asked Anna, surprised to feel a pang of sympathy.

'That's certainly part of it. Losing them both in such a short space of time was pretty devastating. I needed time to myself to mourn them. I was also landed with a job I wasn't trained for. Since the estate manager retired I've worked so damned hard I don't have much inclination for socialising.' He smiled wryly.

'A lot different from life for you at one time,' she commented.

'Too true. In the old days in the City, juggling with other people's millions, I burnt the candle at both ends, never imagining that one day I'd have to take over here. Eddy was the heir; I was just the spare.' He smiled. 'Dominic refers to himself as The Accident.'

'During the very brief time we spent together,' said Anna very deliberately, 'Dominic told me he's doing well at his auction house.'

Ryder acknowledged her barb with a wry smile. 'He'll do even better after he marries the founder's granddaughter.'

'Plus the inheritance you thought I lusted after,' she reminded him tartly. 'Did you really believe I was after Dominic—of all people—for his money?'

Ryder shrugged. 'No point in lying. Until you put me right on the subject, I admit that I did, briefly. I couldn't see what the attraction was otherwise in someone you'd known as a baby.'

'At least you're honest! Didn't your aunt leave you anything?'

'Aunt Augusta said I made too much money of my own to need hers. And she didn't leave Eddy anything because he was the heir to the estate, so Dominic got the lot.'

Anna eyed him searchingly. 'Do you hanker after your old life, Ryder?'

He shook his head. 'Oddly enough, no. I enjoyed the cut and thrust of it at the time, not to mention the money that bought the smart flat and the sexy cars. But secretly I always envied Eddy. I would have exchanged it all in a flash to be in his shoes, running this place.' Ryder smiled bitterly. 'Then suddenly I was doing just that, in the last way I would have chosen. So, Anna Morton, the moral is to be careful what you wish for in case it's granted.'

'Amen to that,' she said soberly as they went downstairs.

'Mr Ryder won't use the dining room these days,' Mrs Carter apologised as Ryder seated Anna at a small table in the morning room.

'This is much cosier,' Anna assured her.

'And much nearer the kitchen,' added Ryder.

They ate perfectly grilled trout with lemon, served with small buttered potatoes and a green salad. Mrs Carter eyed Anna's empty plate with approval when she arrived with their pudding. 'Mr Ryder tells me you've had pneumonia, of all things, a young girl like you, Anna, so you need plenty of good food inside you to make sure you get over it properly. I've put cheese on the side table so I'll just take these plates and leave you in peace.'

'Thank you for a delicious meal,' said Anna warmly. 'This tart looks wonderful.'

'I froze the raspberries myself in the summer, dear, so you enjoy a nice big slice with some cream.' Mrs Carter smiled, pleased, as she bore her tray out of the room.

'You heard what Martha said,' commented Ryder as he served Anna. 'You need to eat.'

'Not hard to do when food like this is put in front of me.' She helped herself to cream.

'I hope you appreciate the eco-friendly menu. The potatoes and raspberries are home-grown and I caught the trout myself last season. That's a very odd look you're giving me,' he added.

'I was just wondering—but it's none of my business,' she added hastily. 'Let's talk about something else.'

He looked down his nose at her. 'Are you wondering, by any chance, if the double death duties left me so stony broke I can't afford to serve a decent meal?'

'No, of course not.' She bit her lip, flushing, wishing now she'd stayed at the cottage, broken window or not.

'The simplicity of the menu,' he said very deliberately, 'is not due to lack of funds, Anna. It's the kind of food we often eat. If I'd known it would worry you, I would have asked Martha to serve lobster and tournedos Rossini.'

Anna put down her fork without tasting the tart. 'Perhaps I should have had supper in my room after all. You know perfectly well I wasn't criticising the menu. And your funds, lack of them or otherwise, don't interest me in the slightest—*Squire*.'

Ryder looked at her in silence for a moment. 'I apologise for the cheap crack, Anna. Please eat the tart or Martha will be upset.'

'I wouldn't upset *Mrs Carter* for the world,' said Anna pointedly and picked up her fork again.

'Point taken,' said Ryder. 'But, just to put the record straight, I'm in a better position than some men who inherit this kind of place, due to the money I'd earned—and invested—in my banking days.' He shrugged. 'It's good to have it as a cushion, I admit, but even without it I'm not destitute. I'm running the estate with the money left after the debts were settled, though I'm doing it rather differently from Eddy.'

'In what way?'

'By seeking new sources of revenue. When your grandfather retired, Eddy was all for selling off the shoots Hector used to organise, but there's good money to be made in that area, so once I've hired a new gamekeeper I shall reinstate them. The facilities for catering are still in the barns and that kind of thing is pretty popular with jaded businessmen at weekends. I've also been approached by a television company to use the house as the setting for a period drama. Eddy would have hated that, but I jumped at the chance of more revenue for the estate.'

Anna nodded. 'Sounds like a good move. By the way, did *you* show my grandfather how to play the market?'

'Guilty as charged,' he admitted. 'Not that he needed much teaching. He was a natural.'

'Do you still do that kind of thing yourself, Ryder?'

'Sometimes, when it's a cast-iron certainty.' He smiled reminiscently. 'I used to worry about Hector, but he'd just smile that slow smile of his and promise to be careful.'

'Did he ever lose much money?'

'To my knowledge he never lost a penny. A canny man, your grandfather.'

'That he was. You know he left me the cottage?'

Ryder nodded. 'He told me when he started the renovations.'

'He left the equivalent in money to Dad and Tom and they're worried that I got the poor deal.' Anna shrugged. 'But I earn enough to cover the running costs of the cottage. I'm a provident sort of female. And, contrary to some people's belief,' she added significantly, 'money has never been my sole interest.'

'Rubbing salt in my wound, Anna?'

'Hard as I can!' She smiled a little. 'Though I shouldn't when you're being so kind, Ryder.'

'The least I could do in the circumstances,' he said, shrugging, and got up. 'Martha will have coffee ready by now, so I'll save her a journey.'

Anna felt a sense of intrusion as she took a good look round the pretty, comfortable room she'd never been in before. The kitchen had been the only territory familiar to her in the old days. Ryder had often taken the young Mortons in there for cake and drinks at the kitchen table, with Dominic delighted to be part of the group while his nanny enjoyed a cup of tea with Mrs Carter. She sighed. It all seemed so long ago, like something in another life.

'What are you thinking about?' asked Ryder, when he came back with a tray.

'I was wallowing in nostalgia. It's funny that Dominic, the youngest, will be the first of us to get married, after all.'

'True. And I'm afraid this is tea, not coffee,' added Ryder. 'Martha thought it would be better for you after your shock.'

'She's absolutely right,' said Anna gratefully. 'I'd love some tea, if you'll pour it.'

'You feel shaky?'

'Not in the least. I'm just afraid to touch that teapot. I saw one just like it valued at a frighteningly high price on one of the antiques programmes the other day.'

'Really?' Ryder eyed the pot with new respect. 'We don't use it normally. Martha obviously thought you merited the best china.'

'I'm honoured!'

'Hannah was the last one to merit the honour. Martha took to her in a big way.'

'I suppose Dominic's getting married in New York?'

'Yes. Though when he brought Hannah on a visit to show her the ancestral home she was so taken with the Manor she was all for having the wedding in the village church with a reception right here at the house. But her parents, naturally enough, wanted her to be married from her own home.' Ryder eyed her speculatively. 'Talking of weddings, why aren't you married yet, Anna?'

She shrugged. 'Mr Right hasn't shown up yet.'

'But you lived with someone for quite a time. Hector used to keep me up to speed when I saw him.'

'Did he also tell you he disapproved? To him it was living in sin.' Anna pulled a face. 'In actual fact it was nothing so exciting. Sean and I both worked such long hours we gradually saw less and less of each other. Eventually I discovered that we had totally different ideas about our relationship, so I moved out.'

'Did he come here often?'

'No. I preferred to visit Gramp on my own. You met Sean during the only weekend he ever came to the cottage. It never stopped raining and he never stopped complaining—not least because I insisted he slept in the spare bedroom. Gramp didn't take to him, and not long after that I moved out of Sean's flat.'

Ryder raised an eyebrow. 'Because Hector didn't approve?'

'It was a contributory factor,' she admitted. 'They never said so, but I know Dad and Tom weren't hugely keen either. But now I share a flat with Clare Saunders, someone my entire family approves of. Gramp took to Clare in a big way when she came to Keeper's not so long ago.'

'I met them when they were out for a walk.' He looked at her. 'You'd stayed behind. To avoid me, no doubt.'

'Yes,' she said frankly. 'Gramp was keen to show Clare round the estate. I hope you didn't mind.'

'You really need to ask that?'

Her eyes kindled. 'I wouldn't have done once. But after the accusations you made I felt I didn't know you any more.'

'When I discovered my mistake I made sincere apologies,' he reminded her coldly. 'Since you flatly refused to accept them, I see no point in apologising again.'

'Message received, Ryder.' She got to her feet. 'Thank you for supper, and for coming to my rescue. I'm a bit tired, so I'll say goodnight.'

'I'll see you to your room,' said Ryder, and walked upstairs with her in a silence he kept up until they reached the door of the blue room. 'I hope you sleep well, Anna.'

'Me, too,' she said fervently.

He opened the door. 'If you have nightmares about intruders, just yell. My room's across the landing.'

'Thank you. Goodnight.' Anna closed the door, glad that someone would be close at hand in this big, empty house with its elegant high-ceilinged rooms. She'd been upstairs at the Manor occasionally when she was young, but only on rainy afternoons when Ryder sneaked her up the back stairs with Tom to his old room on the floor above. Now Ryder probably slept in state in the master bedroom that had been off limits to him in the old days.

The bed was comfortable, but Anna had no great hopes of a restful night after an evening that had been a strain from start to finish. And, added to that, she felt guilty about ringing Ryder instead of her father or Tom. It was only because Ryder was the nearest, she argued to herself, but that was only partly true. In spite of their differences, she'd had no hesitation in turning to him for help.

Ryder Wyndham had always been the ultimate hero to her—from the day she first met him, right up to the moment when he came crashing down from his pedestal. But tonight he'd come straight to her rescue and taken over with efficiency she couldn't fault. If she was going to spend time at the cottage in future, it would be inconvenient to go on harbouring a grudge—much better to remember the casual, taken-for-granted friendship they'd shared as children. But in those days she had been blissfully ignorant of the social differences between them. Now, supposedly classless society or not, the gulf between the gamekeeper's granddaughter and the Squire still yawned as wide as ever, as Ryder had proved beyond all doubt when he thought she had ambitions to marry into his family.

Anna woke to sunshine and a knock on the door.

'Are you decent?' called Ryder.

She scrambled upright, flipping her braid over her shoulder as she yanked the quilt up to her chin. 'Yes.'

The door opened slowly as Ryder backed in with a tray. 'Good morning. I saved Martha a trip.'

'I would have come down,' Anna protested as he laid the tray across her lap. And would have made sure she looked rather more appetising before she had.

'Martha says you need looking after,' said Ryder, shrugging.

Anna looked through a sudden mist of tears at the perfectly poached egg and crisp triangles of wholemeal toast.

'Anna!' Ryder stared at her in surprise. 'You don't have to eat the egg if you don't want to.'

'I do, I do,' she said, sniffing inelegantly. 'Sorry. It's just that Mrs Carter's so kind and—'

'And you've had a shock and you're grieving for Hector.' The unexpected sympathy in his voice almost started her off again.

'He always poached an egg for me when I was under the weather.'

Ryder went into the bathroom and came back with a handful of tissues. 'Mop yourself up and try to eat something, if only to please Martha.'

'Of course I will,' said Anna, blowing her nose. 'Sorry to be such a drama queen.'

'Good girl. Martha will be up with some tea when you've finished.'

Good girl, thought Anna derisively as she began on her breakfast. Ryder behaved as though he were thirty years older than her, instead of just three. But from now on she must try hard to be less hostile, she reminded herself, for Gramp's sake if nothing else. Hector Morton had been very fond of the Wyndham boys, Ryder most of all.

Mrs Carter arrived with a cup of tea and a bag of clean laundry just as Anna was finishing the last piece of toast. 'That's the way,' she said, beaming in approval. 'I didn't want Mr Ryder to disturb you so early, but he said you'd be keen to get back to the cottage to put things straight before your father arrives.'

'He's absolutely right,' said Anna with feeling. 'But thank you so much for the laundry, and my delicious breakfast. I'll just drink some tea, then I'll get dressed. Would you tell Ryder I'd be grateful for a lift back in about half an hour?'

'Very well, dear. Your bits of underwear are all fresh and clean and aired overnight on the Aga,' said Mrs Carter, putting the bag on the bed. 'You need to take care of yourself, Anna. You still look peaky to me.'

'I'm fine, honestly, Mrs C.' She pulled a face. 'I have to be. I'm due back in work soon.'

Ryder was waiting in the kitchen when Anna got downstairs. He took her bag, waited while she said her goodbyes and then helped her up into the Land Rover.

'Martha's very worried about you,' he stated as he drove off. 'In her opinion you need to look a lot better before you can even think of going back to such a demanding job.'

'Someone else might snaffle my demanding job if I don't get back to it soon.'

'Would that be such a tragedy?'

'Not a tragedy exactly, but I'm good at what I do and it pays well. Now I'm a home-owner I need the money to keep my property up to scratch.'

'Don't worry about Keeper's Cottage,' said Ryder quickly. 'I'll make sure word gets out that I'm keeping an eye on it until the repairs are done.'

Anna shot him a startled look. 'Heavens, I never thought about repairs. I'd better get something sorted before Dad arrives.'

'How long is he staying?'

'Just for lunch. He's going back this afternoon.'

'Then we'd better get a move on to inspect the damage.'

She shook her head decisively. 'You needn't stay to help me, Ryder! You've done more than enough already.'

'That's your phone,' he said, ignoring her.

She fished it from her bag to read the text message. 'It's from Dad. He can't make it today. He'll ring later. Oh, well,' she said philosophically, 'that gives me more time to organise repairs. In which case I needn't take up any more of your time, Ryder. I'm sure you have loads of things you should be doing.'

'None of them more important than making sure you're safe on your own in that house,' he said flatly.

Anna shot a glance at his obdurate profile. She remembered that look well enough to know it was useless to argue. 'I'm really very grateful for your help,' she said at last.

Ryder shrugged. 'Hector asked me to look out for you.'

'So that's why you're doing it! You're afraid he'll haunt you if you don't.'

He shook his head, keeping his eyes on the ruts in the lane. 'I'm doing it for your sake as well as his. When we were children you were like a little sister to me—or maybe another brother, because in those days I never really thought of you as a girl.' Ryder shot her a sidelong glance. 'In spite of what's happened between us since, the connection's still there, Anna. You need help. I can provide it. It's as simple as that.'

CHAPTER FOUR

RYDER dropped Anna off at the cottage, then took off again to fetch something from the village. When he got back he walked straight past her with a television he set down on the vacant stand in the parlour.

'Did you buy that for me?' she demanded, bristling. 'Tell me how much and I'll pay.'

He frowned impatiently. 'It's not a diamond necklace, Anna—it's not even new. Brian James does them up in his spare time. Look on it as a present.'

'Then thank you. It's very kind of you,' she added belatedly. She really needed another television. 'Who's Brian James?'

'His father runs the garage in the village. Brian's a local builder, but he can turn his hand to practically anything. He should be on his way by now to view the damage, so keep a look out for him while I heave mattresses around.'

Anna spotted a white van at the gate as she was finishing up in the parlour. She switched off the vacuum cleaner and called up to Ryder. 'I think your man's here.'

Ryder ran downstairs to open the door. 'Be gentle with him, Anna. He's a bit shy.'

'Thank you for coming at such short notice, Mr James,' she said warmly as the young man reached them.

'No problem,' he said, flushing.

'Good man,' said Ryder, taking the box Brian gave him. 'In

my opinion Miss Morton needs an efficient alarm system, new locks on all the windows and the two outer doors and a replacement pane of glass in the smallest bedroom, plus a new window ledge and some plastering on the wall below it. Miss Morton will take you up to have a look while I set the television up, and then come down and give me your opinion.'

'What's in that box?' asked Anna suspiciously, after she'd left Brian upstairs assessing the damage.

'Something else you need.' Ryder handed it over, then stretched out on the floor to deal with plugs and sockets at the back of the television.

She laughed as she took out a new kettle. 'Now this I'm *really* grateful for!'

'I thought you might be.' Ryder got to his feet, switched on the television, scrolled through the programmes, then switched it off again and handed her the remote control. 'All yours.'

'Thanks a lot, Ryder.' She eyed him warily. 'Sorry I was so ungrateful just now. It would have been a bit quiet here tonight without a television.'

He shrugged. 'My thoughts exactly. Make up for your ingratitude by putting the new kettle on for coffee.'

While he drank his coffee, Brian gave them a rough estimate for the work needed. Anna, secretly amazed that the figure was so reasonable, asked him how soon he could start and, after arranging to begin the following Monday, Brian took off in his van. Anna immediately set to work, aided, to her astonishment, by Ryder, no matter how much she protested that she could manage perfectly well on her own.

'I was asked to keep an eye on you,' he reminded her. 'In my book that doesn't mean allowing you to exhaust yourself to the point of getting ill again.'

Anna opened her mouth to protest, then, at the steely look in Ryder's eyes, she closed it again and got to work.

Due to their combined efforts the cottage was soon immaculate again, but by that time Anna felt so weary she had to acknowledge that she couldn't have done it all so quickly on her own.

'Have you got anything to eat?' Ryder demanded, stretching. 'I'll have far more respect for Martha and her crew in future. This cleaning business is hungry work.'

'Won't Mrs Carter have your lunch waiting?' she said, surprised.

'No. When I took over the reins I established a new routine, which means I fend for myself at weekends unless I've got someone coming to dinner. She spends hers with her gentleman friend.'

Anna's eyes widened. 'Really? Good for her!'

'Martha was embarrassed when she told me about the arrangement, but I was only too happy she had company.'

'Why was she embarrassed?'

Ryder shrugged. 'She lives in an estate cottage and thought I had a right to know, God knows why.'

'Have you met her friend?'

'Yes. Pleasant chap. A bit younger than Martha, but no harm in that.'

She sniffed. 'You've changed your tune!'

His face darkened. 'It was a hell of a lot different where you and Dominic were concerned.'

'Don't I know it! You thought I was the wrong bride for him in every possible way.'

He shook his head, a wry twist to his mouth. 'I thought Dominic was totally wrong for you, Anna. There's a difference.'

She thrust a hand through her hair, yawning. 'If there is, I feel too tired to work out what it is right now.'

'No wonder. You're exhausted. You just had to get the whole house in shape today, of course,' he said, exasperated. 'You were always an obstinate little mule.'

'I couldn't rest until all trace of my burglar was gone.' Anna sighed in frustration. 'It's such a drag to feel like this, Ryder. Normally I work long and hard and go out most evenings, and now just the thought of any of it makes me tired.'

'No surprise after working non-stop all morning. You need a rest.'

'And you need food,' she said briskly. 'I did some shopping yesterday—was it only yesterday? It seems ages ago.'

'And now you can recline gracefully on a sofa while I make lunch with whatever I find.'

'Certainly not, Ryder. I can—'

'No, you most definitely cannot.' The blue eyes were adamant. 'Tom asked me to take care of you and I promised him I would.'

She scowled at him. 'You know I can't argue when you put it like that.'

'Whatever works! Sit down and try out the new television while I make lunch.'

'Oh, all right. But just a sandwich, Ryder. Any kind you like.' Anna left him to it and curled up on the sofa, depressed because she needed a rest so badly.

When Ryder came back with a tray, she smiled in awe at the vast quantity of sandwiches. 'These look good. And so many of them!'

'I'm hungry. I used my initiative about fillings,' he added, sitting opposite. 'The tins were Hector's?'

Anna nodded. 'He was the all-time carnivore. No tuna or sardines for him.' She eyed the sandwich she picked up. 'What's in here with my lettuce? I didn't buy any ham.'

'Guess.' Ryder watched, grinning, as she took a bite.

'Spam!' she said, laughing. 'I didn't notice any in the cupboards.'

'I found a tin tucked out of sight at the back. I was always envious when Hector gave you Spam sandwiches for picnics.'

'And I always swapped for some of whatever you had,' she reminded him.

'I know. You were a good pal.' Ryder helped himself and sat back on the other sofa with his plate, looking so much at home Anna asked him if this was something he'd done before.

He nodded. 'I called in on your grandfather a lot, sometimes to ask his invaluable advice, but often just to sit and reminisce for a while over a beer in the evening.' He gave her a sardonic smile. 'I not only enjoyed Hector's company, it was a good way to get news of you, Anna.'

'Gramp talked about me?' She took another bite of sandwich to hide her surprise. 'He never told me.'

'You were his favourite topic of conversation.'

Anna made a face. 'That must have been boring.'

'I wanted to keep track of you after you had cut yourself out of my life so comprehensively. Once I was living here on a permanent basis I thought about you a lot. You and Tom were part of growing up, Anna. School holidays wouldn't have been the same without you.' He shot her a searching look. 'But after I went to university you didn't come here much. Why?'

'I went on package holidays with girlfriends instead, and Gramp was semi-retired by then, so we coaxed him to spend more time in Shrewsbury with us.' Anna tucked a bright tress of hair behind her ear, wondering whether to confess the rest.

His eyes narrowed. 'You're shaping up to tell me something I won't like.'

'Your eighteenth birthday party put me off coming here at all for ages.'

'Why? What happened? Did someone get out of line?'

'If you mean one of the boys, no.' Anna grimaced. 'The girls were the problem. The moment I arrived, one look at that glossy bunch told me my hair was all wrong, my dress even worse. But Edwina French delivered the *coup de grâce*. She made very sure I overheard her wondering what on earth possessed you to invite the gamekeeper's brat.'

'Good God, I wish I'd known!' Ryder put down a half-eaten sandwich, his face grim. 'My reason for inviting you was simple, Anna—I wanted you there. And I thought you looked cute that night. I'd never seen you in a dress before. It was a shock to see you so grown up. But you did a Cinderella act and ran away before midnight, and I had to come chasing after you.'

She nodded. 'The ride in your new car was the highlight of my evening.'

He frowned. 'Did Edwina spoil it for you early on?'

'That was only part of it, Ryder. Your parents were very kind to me, as usual. But when I saw you there among friends from your own background the gulf between us suddenly opened up like the Grand Canyon. It changed everything for me.'

'So that's it. I couldn't understand why you avoided me like the plague afterwards. We met so rarely I had to monitor your progress through Hector.'

'He kept me up-to-date with yours from time to time too. Or as much of it as he thought fit for my innocent young ears! Tom filled in the details about the constant stream of girlfriends.' She looked him in the eye. 'But after you got engaged to Edwina I refused to listen.'

He grimaced. 'Anna, I thought the affair with Edwina was just a casual fling like the others. But she'd been doing the rounds for quite a while by that stage and decided it was time she got married. Our families were neighbours, close friends since way back, so when Edwina told me she was pregnant that was that. But the engagement was a nine day wonder.'

Anna frowned. 'When Tom told me it was all off I was surprised. Surely Edwina would have been delighted to be lady of the manor!'

'She was so utterly delighted I found it pretty hard to take considering I was grieving for my brother. But Eddy had always said that it was up to Dominic and me to provide future Wyndhams, so I consoled myself that at least I would have an heir to look forward to. Aren't you going to ask what went wrong?' he added bitterly.

'Only if you want to tell me.'

'Due to Eddy's death, and the fact that Edwina was pregnant, I suggested we get married very quietly and settle down to running the estate,' said Ryder. His eyes hardened. 'This didn't appeal to Edwina in the slightest. She wanted the wedding of the year followed by the same life we'd led before in London, with just the occasional weekend at the Manor to "keep an eye on things". There was no problem about waiting for a bigger wedding, she assured me blithely, because there was no baby yet. That was just her way of hurrying things up between us. She would have been pregnant sooner or later anyway, she pointed out. She really couldn't see why I was making such a fuss about her little white lie.'

Anna winced. 'So you sent her packing.'

'A move which caused a great deal of unpleasantness at a time when I could have done without it,' he said with deep distaste. 'It was at this point that Dominic came back from visiting you in London and went on about you ad nauseam. He practically salivated as he described you. And because he kept disappearing off to London to spend time with friends before he went back to New York, I assumed that you were the one he was seeing.'

'As I've said before, he came just once to say a brief goodbye,' said Anna wearily.

'I know that now, but at least you see now why I found it only too easy to believe him when he said you were going to marry him.'

She glared at him. 'I still find it incredible—and downright offensive—that you thought I was after your baby brother for his cash.'

'I was not in a rational state of mind at the time.' Ryder looked at her levelly. 'And I thought you were still living with Mansell. I assumed you'd thrown him over in favour of my brother.'

She glared at him, incensed. 'Did you really! Just so you know, it was all over with Sean by then. It ended not long after the weekend I brought him down here to the cottage. We met you in the village.'

'I remember it well. He was trying to rush you home and you were so obviously objecting that I wanted to intervene, but common sense prevailed.' He shrugged. 'After all, he was the man in possession.'

Anna shook her head irritably. 'Sean's role in my life was nothing remotely like that. The weekend down here together proved it, once and for all.'

He nodded grimly. 'I didn't hear you'd left him until much later, otherwise I might have come to you for some sympathy after the break-up with Edwina. In the meantime, Dominic rang from New York and I misheard "Hannah" for "Anna" and believed you were going to marry him and the rest is history.' Ryder looked her in the eye. 'Anna, I tried to make amends afterwards, but your grandfather told me you'd come round in the end.'

'Come round to what, exactly?'

He shrugged, his eyes suddenly inscrutable. 'To being friends again. What else?'

'What you really wanted was someone to make soothing noises after the break-up with Edwina French!'

He smiled sardonically. 'It would have helped.'

'You had a lucky escape,' said Anna firmly.

'True. But when I came to see you that night I was at an all-time low.'

'Then why wouldn't you believe me?' she demanded. 'You'd always been such a hero to me, Ryder. When you hurled those accusations at me I felt so sick it's a wonder I didn't throw up on you.'

His mouth twisted. 'Your eyes haunted me afterwards. I felt like a murderer.'

'You were,' she retorted bitterly. 'You murdered my illusions. I wouldn't let Gramp mention your name afterwards.'

'But Hector had a plan to get round that. He asked me to join you all at the Red Lion for his birthday lunch, but I landed myself in Casualty in the local hospital instead with a broken wrist.' He eyed her challengingly. 'Your father and Tom came over to check on me at home that evening, but not you.'

'No fear! Gramp tried to persuade me to go with them, but I'm an unforgiving soul.' Her eyes danced suddenly as they met his. 'At the time I rather relished the idea of Ryder Wyndham in pain. Eat that last sandwich,' she added. 'My capacity for Spam is smaller now I'm an adult.'

'So is mine,' he said with regret, and got up to take the tray. 'I'll make you some tea.'

Anna jumped up. 'You don't have to wait on me, Ryder.'

His eyes gleamed. 'I thought you'd relish seeing me do humble!'

She laughed. 'I would. But I fancy coffee, not tea, and I'll make it myself.'

'I can help—'

'No room. The kitchen may be smarter these days, but it's still small.'

Anna was glad of the brief respite alone after Ryder's revelations. At one time he'd been the best friend she'd ever had, then suddenly her enemy. She was having a hard time keeping up now it was all changed again.

'So, Anna.' His eyes were searching when she returned with the coffee. 'How do you feel now you know the truth?'

'I don't know,' she said candidly. 'You haven't been part of my life for a long time now.'

He picked up his mug and sat down opposite her. 'You were the one who made sure that I didn't see much of you over the years. Not that I was neglected. In my City days there was no shortage of girlfriends because I had money and reasonable looks—'

'Reasonable! That hair of yours was outrageous.' She shook her head. 'I hardly recognised you all sober and shorn the night you came to the flat.'

'It was nothing to do with my haircut. I was angry.'

'Hard to miss that!'

He nodded. 'Anyway, to keep to the subject, it was *your* hair that amazed me when I met you that day with Mansell. You kept it so short when you were young.'

'After your party I let it grow. I've never had more than half an inch cut off it since.' She frowned. 'But we met now and again when our visits here coincided. You must have noticed my hair, Ryder.'

'Not the way it was that day. Your scarf blew off and that hair streamed in the wind like a gold banner. For the first time I realised that my little friend had grown into a very attractive woman.' He smiled grimly. 'The shock of it put rather a damper on my social graces.'

'I thought you were plain hostile.' She smiled a little. 'I was so quiet afterwards Gramp thought I was coming down with something after our soaking. But it was Sean who caught cold.'

'In more ways than one if you left him afterwards!' Ryder looked her in the eye. 'So, Anna Morton, shall we call a truce or are you still hostile towards me?'

'Not hostile exactly,' she said with caution. 'It's just hard for me to get past the gulf between us, Ryder. You're still the Squire and I'm still Hector Morton's granddaughter.'

'That has certainly never bothered Tom, so surely we can be friends again, Anna.' His face shadowed. 'Just between you and me, I do miss female company.'

She shook her head, unmoved. 'Oh, come *on*, Ryder. There must be a lot of women in the neighbourhood only too happy to do something about that.'

'True. But no one I'm particularly attracted to.'

She eyed him curiously. 'What do you do about sex, then?'

He gave a shout of laughter. 'You were never one for beating about the bush, Anna. I had a devil of a time trying to answer your questions when we were kids. In this case the answer's simple—hard work and, as the last resort, cold showers.'

Anna flushed, wishing she'd kept her mouth shut. 'I suppose that's one of the ways women differ from men. Since I split up with Sean, I don't miss the sex part at all.'

'There must have been other men in your life since?'

'I've been working so hard lately, my socialising tends to be a drink after work with a crowd of other people, plus the occasional party and a trip to the cinema now and then with Clare or one of my friends from the office. Frankly,' she added, shrugging, 'romantic relationships are too much work.'

'Probably because you work too hard otherwise, according to your father. You need to slow down a bit, Anna.'

'Dad tends to worry about me because my mother died of pneumonia. But my constitution is a lot tougher than hers ever was. You know that. I never lagged behind you and Tom when we were young.'

He snorted. 'Far from it. You were never ready to call it a day.'

'Bossy little darling, wasn't I?' Anna smiled reminiscently. 'Did the sun really shine every day in those summers?'

'Of course not. It rained a lot too. We spent quite a few afternoons up in my room, remember.' Ryder's eyes gleamed. 'You're the only female who ever shared my bedroom at the Manor.'

'Tom came too!' Anna eyed him in surprise. 'But surely Edwina must have passed through the sacred portal now and again?'

Ryder shook his head. 'Our engagement was brief and Eddy very starchy about that kind of thing, so she never slept with me at the Manor. I knew very well that he didn't care for her. And when Dominic got home to find Edwina was history he was brutally honest about his relief. But because things were pretty bad all round at the time for me, he hadn't the heart to tell me about his own happy-ever-after plans right away. He waited until he got back to New York.'

'It still amazes me that you could ever imagine I'd marry Dominic,' said Anna, shaking her head. 'At one time I even changed his nappies, for heaven's sake. And please don't bring up the wretched money again. A man doesn't need money to attract me, so let's get that straight from the start. If we are to be friends again it's nothing to do with your worldly goods, Ryder.'

He nodded soberly. 'I hope it's due to the rapport we once had. I've never found it with anyone else.'

Neither had Anna, but she wasn't about to tell him that. 'I wonder if you'd do me a favour, Ryder, or do you have to get back?'

'No, I don't,' he assured her. 'What sort of favour?'

'I'd like to save Dad the hassle of going through Gramp's things to look for the gold hunter. But I don't fancy doing it on my own.'

'Of course I'll help.' He stood up. 'Afterwards you can have supper with me.'

'Where?'

'My place. Martha always leaves me enough food for a siege.'

'In that case, thank you, I will. For an awful moment I thought you were going to ask me to cook,' she said flippantly. Or suggest dinner at the Red Lion. Eating out with the Squire at any time would cause comment, but so soon after her grandfather's death would set local tongues wagging at both ends. Bad idea if she intended regular visits to Keeper's Cottage. 'If you'll follow me, then.'

It was a poignant experience to look through Hector Morton's clothes, but none of his tweeds, or the sober dark suit worn to church, yielded up the watch. Ryder searched through the drawers he'd replaced earlier and Anna went through the blankets in the ottoman at the foot of the bed, then said something rude as a splinter stuck in her finger.

'Let me see,' said Ryder, kneeling beside her.

Anna held out her forefinger and Ryder took it in his mouth, sucking hard on the spot where the splinter had pierced the skin. She looked down at his thick, curling hair, startled to find that his sucking mouth was affecting a lot more of her than just her finger. She snatched it away and scrambled to her feet. 'I'm sure it'll be fine,' she said gruffly, eyeing the puncture on her fingertip. 'It's gone. Have you swallowed it?'

Ryder touched the tip of his tongue to the back of his hand as he got up and showed her the tiny sliver of wood. 'There's the culprit.'

'Thank you. I hate splinters.'

'Nothing in the ottoman, then.'

'No,' she said disconsolately. 'Dad will be terribly upset. I've searched every inch of my room, but no luck. Not that I expected it.'

'Have you checked the spare room?'

'I didn't think there was much point. Gramp wouldn't have kept it in there.'

'Having gone this far, we might as well make sure.'

The likelihood of hiding places in the spare room seemed remote at first glance. A chair stood at the foot of each twin bed and a table between them, but otherwise a cupboard built into an alcove was the only piece of furniture.

'That's always left empty for Dad and Tom to use,' said Anna, eyeing the broken window gloomily. No chance of a good night's sleep until that was mended.

Ryder switched on the main light and looked in the cupboard. 'It's not old enough to date from when the cottage was built, but it's pretty ancient, just the same. There might be some kind of secret drawer.'

Ryder opened the doors and removed the row of shelves fitted on one side of the hanging space. He rapped the interior with his knuckles, but shook his head. 'Solid everywhere.' He turned round to find Anna examining the shelves lined up on the floor.

She tapped one with her fingernail. 'This one's a bit smaller inside.'

Ryder picked it up and put it on the bed. 'You're right.'

'But I doubt that Gramp would have hidden his watch in there.'

'I could prise the back away to make sure. But I'll need a screwdriver.'

'Downstairs in the pantry. I'll get it.' Anna ran downstairs to the cupboard under the pantry sink and heaved out a battered red tool box, pulled the two halves apart and took out a selection of screwdrivers upstairs to Ryder, out of breath as she brandished the tools. 'I—brought a—choice,' she gasped as she slumped on the bed.

'For heaven's sake, Anna, take it easy!'

'I'm fine.' She pushed at his arm. 'Go *on*, Ryder.'

He inserted the tip of a screwdriver into one side of the back section, then smiled in triumph as the thin slab of wood at the back of the drawer fell into the drawer to reveal a flat tin box set flush behind it. Ryder prised it out with care and handed it to Anna. She raised the lid eagerly, then sighed in disappointment as she found a thin bundle of yellowed lined paper tied with ribbon so faded it was impossible to make out the original colour.

CHAPTER FIVE

'NO WATCH,' said Anna disconsolately. 'No envelopes either, but these are obviously letters. Want to read them with me?'

They were addressed to dearest Violet and signed by an obviously adoring Ned, who wrote in an educated hand, telling her how beautiful she was and how much he treasured her letters and the magical hours spent with her on his last leave. The notes were brief but eloquent, each one ending with poignant avowals of love all the more powerful for their restraint. The final letter was dated 18th March 1918.

'Ned obviously didn't make it home,' said Ryder at last.

'No.' Anna drew in a deep, unsteady breath. 'So poor Violet closed the box and hid them away. That's so *sad*. I wonder who she was.'

'If she lived in Keeper's Cottage there must be records in the estate office. We'll look them up.' Ryder got up and held out his hand to pull her to her feet. 'I'm sorry about the watch, Anna.'

'Compared with Violet's loss, that doesn't seem such a big thing any more,' she said soberly.

'Come on,' he ordered. 'Lock up and come back with me for the evening.'

'I need a bath first.' Anna smiled at him. 'You go on; I'll drive up later.'

* * *

Ryder felt better on the drive home than he had for some time. After Anna's furious rejection of his attempts to apologise, coming so soon after the debacle with Edwina, he'd thought to hell with all women and eventually convinced himself that Anna Morton no longer mattered to him as a friend or in any other capacity. But when he saw her throwing snowdrops on her grandfather's coffin his heart had contracted at the sight of her so pale and fragile in her elegant mourning black. It had been hard to believe that this Anna, grown-up and grieving, had once been the sunburned little tomboy who'd left such a gap in his life when she removed herself from it. Spending time with her again had brought home to him just how much he'd missed the only female in his life he'd ever looked on as a friend.

Ryder went straight to the kitchen to take a casserole from the refrigerator; wondering if chicken with vegetables was Anna's kind of thing. Always supposing she turned up to eat it, he thought wryly. But whether he had company for dinner or not, he needed a shower and a change of clothes. By the time he was ready in jeans and blue herringbone shirt he was feeling increasing enthusiasm for Martha's casserole. He towelled his hair dry, thrust his fingers through it, pulled a dark red sweater over the shirt and ran downstairs, past the family portraits which had so impressed Miss Hannah Breckenridge on her recent visit to her fiancé's ancestral home. As he reached the hall he heard a car approaching and ran into the kitchen to throw open the door.

'You made it,' Ryder said, helping Anna out of the car.

'Am I late, then?'

'No. But you might have sent me on ahead so you could think up an excuse not to turn up.'

Anna stared at him in surprise as they went inside. 'Why should you think that?'

'Recent experience.' Ryder eyed her appreciatively as he took her jacket. 'You look good, Anna.'

Anna smiled her thanks. Not for the world would she have

let him know she'd spent ages over her hair and face and dithered like a teenager over her limited selection of clothes. She wasn't sure why she'd fussed so much! But from the look in Ryder's eyes, her black jeans, white shirt and shell-pink sweater had obviously been a good choice. 'I took time for a chat with Dad before I set out, but I didn't mention the break-in. I'd rather get the cottage sorted before I tell him. I checked up on Clare too. She's got a really ferocious cold, poor thing.'

'Then you can't go back to the flat yet,' said Ryder as they made for the kitchen. 'Would you mind sitting here while I perform miracles with a microwave?'

'Not in the least.' Anna looked round with nostalgia. 'I always loved this kitchen. Are we going to eat here?'

'It would be a lot easier for the chef if we do.'

'Right. What can I do to help?'

Ryder set the timer on the microwave and put plates and silverware on the table. 'You sort these. I'll cut bread and open the wine.'

When they were seated opposite each other at the big table with steaming bowls in front of them, Anna smiled across at Ryder and sipped some of the fruity red wine in her glass. 'Fast food at its best,' Anna said, then frowned a little as she looked round the room. 'Where's the Aga?'

'I don't have one.'

'But Mrs Carter said she aired my laundry on the Aga overnight.'

'Ah.' Ryder grinned. 'She meant the one in her own kitchen. Martha stayed later last night because you were here, but normally she goes home at six. I thought you might refuse to sleep here if you knew.'

Anna stared at him, her fork halfway to her mouth. 'Why?'

He leered theatrically. 'Because we'd be alone here overnight, fair maiden.'

She shook her head, laughing. 'Ryder, this is the new millennium. In the unlikely event that the Squire wanted his evil way with me, the presence of Mrs Carter would hardly have been a deterrent.'

'You weren't eager to come,' he reminded her. 'I thought you'd refuse point blank if I told you Martha went home every night.'

'Actually, you're wrong,' she said, wiping crusty bread round her bowl. 'I would have come anyway rather than sleep—or not sleep—at the cottage last night. Stupid, really. The burglar was hardly likely to come back.' She popped a morsel of bread in her mouth, her eyes sparkling. 'Dear me, Ryder, did you tell Mrs Carter to *lie*?'

'Certainly not,' he retorted. 'It was pure luck that she didn't let the cat out of the bag.' He pushed the casserole towards her. 'Have some more.'

'I don't think I can.' She smiled at him hopefully. 'But if there's any raspberry tart left I could make room for that.'

After everything was cleared away afterwards to Anna's satisfaction, Ryder took her into the morning room.

'It's early yet,' said Ryder, 'unless you have a burning desire to get back to Keeper's Cottage right away, Anna.'

It was the last thing she wanted. 'None at all. I love this room too,' she told him as she curled up on a sofa in front of the fireplace. 'I was never allowed in here in the old days.'

'Neither was I much.' Ryder knelt to put a match to the kindling under the logs. 'This was my mother's private territory.'

'I adored your mother. She was always so kind to me.'

'She felt great sympathy for you and Tom when your mother died. You more than Tom, she told me years later, because there are certain times when a girl needs a mother and a father won't do.'

Ryder sat down beside her. 'Remember when you plagued me to smuggle you into the stables when a stallion arrived to cover Eddy's mare? You bombarded me with questions which embarrassed the hell out of me.' He shook his head. 'I was red as fire all over, Tom too, but you wouldn't budge until my father came to throw us out.'

Anna shook her head, chuckling. 'I didn't believe a word of it when you said it was more or less the same procedure for humans. I told Gramp you'd been telling horrible lies when I went home. I was so disgusted when he said it was true, I made a vow. If that's what people did to get babies I wasn't having any, ever.'

Ryder got up to put more logs on the fire. 'Presumably you changed your mind at some point.'

'About the procedure, yes, but not the babies.'

Ryder sat down again and gazed into the fire. 'Just as well if you're so wrapped up in your career.'

'At the moment I'm not. They rang from the firm yesterday, to ask when I was getting back, and I said I needed a bit longer to convalesce.' Anna sighed. 'They probably think I'm malingering.'

'Be sensible, Anna,' he said impatiently. 'You're not up to it yet.'

'I know. To be honest, Ryder, I was scared silly when I woke with a raging temperature and pains knifing through my chest. Lucky for me, Clare ignored my protests, called a doctor and I was in an ambulance on the way to hospital before I could draw breath—which was getting harder to do by the minute.'

'It must have been a hell of a shock for your father and Tom,' he said soberly. 'Hector told me you had a dose of flu like his.'

'I did initially, but like an idiot I went back to work too soon. It was my own stupid fault that I landed myself in hospital.' Anna's eyes filled. 'And while I was there it was Gramp who died, not me.'

Ryder moved closer. 'But he lived to a very good age, Anna, and enjoyed his life to the full.'

'I know. And I'm passionately grateful for that. But he died so suddenly it just hasn't sunk in yet that he's gone.' She blew her nose and tried to smile. 'Sorry, Ryder. I'm depressing you.'

'No, you're not. I'm happy to listen, any time you want,' he assured her, and put an arm round her. 'That's what friends are for.' Except that friendship wasn't quite the word for his feelings now he'd been fool enough to make such close contact. Shaken by his unexpected reaction to contact with Anna's body, he took his arm away and got up to poke the fire.

'My father can't make it this weekend, by the way,' Anna said when he sat down again. 'One of his colleagues is off sick and Dad's on call in his place.'

'Spend Sunday here with me, then,' said Ryder casually. 'If the weather's good we can take a trip down memory lane and visit our old haunts. If it rains we search for Violet and Ned in the archives.'

Anna liked the sound of that. 'What would you normally do?'

'Get up a bit later than usual and apply myself to the dreaded paperwork and various odd jobs, but I'll take be glad to take a day off.'

'Then thanks, I'd like that. I'll cook lunch if you like.'

'With your house in its present state I think you should stay the night again,' he said quickly.

She sighed, sorely tempted. 'I mustn't let that wretched burglar turn me into a coward.'

'It's only sensible,' he urged. 'You can move back in once Brian does the repairs. You'll feel more up to it by then.'

Anna doubted that but she let herself be persuaded. 'All right.'

'So, how about a drink?'

'No thanks. I had two glasses of wine earlier, remember. I'm happy as I am. Ryder, do you think I should sell?' she added suddenly.

'No. Your grandfather went to a lot of trouble to do the cottage up for you, so hang on to it.' And without it she'd have no reason for coming back here.

'You're right,' she agreed and lapsed into comfortable silence again. After a while she turned her head round to look up at him. 'Could I have a tour of the house some time?'

'Any time you like.'

'Thank you. I've always wanted to explore Wyndham Manor.'

'You could have done that any time you liked since I took over.'

'We haven't exactly been on speaking terms, Ryder.'

'But we're friends again now.' He looked down into her upturned face. 'Agreed?'

Anna looked up into the intent blue eyes for a moment, then nodded. 'Agreed. Come on then, *friend*. Let's explore your freezer and see what we can find for Sunday lunch.'

Ryder took her back through the kitchen into an adjoining room she'd never ventured into before.

'What a huge utility room,' said Anna, awed.

'Known here as the scullery,' said Ryder, opening a freezer. 'What do you fancy?'

'Something easy. Joints of meat don't feature in my life.'

Ryder pulled out a drawer marked 'Use First' and looked through the contents. 'Pork loin, brisket of beef—'

'That's the one,' said Anna promptly. 'Gramp used to do it quite often. He just put it in a pot with a lid and cooked it slowly.'

Once the joint was unwrapped and left to defrost they went back to the morning room, but this time Ryder kept his distance when they sat down on the sofa.

'You'd better not tell Mrs Carter what you've been up to today,' she remarked. 'She'd have a fit if she knew the Squire had been helping me clean my house.'

He shot her a gleaming blue look. 'I won't tell her. Though I'd have you know it's not a first for me. I was a student once, remember.'

'But don't try and kid me you didn't have a cleaner for your famous loft!'

'I won't, because I did. But she took holidays, just like anyone else.'

'Surely one of the girlfriends could have helped out?'

Ryder hooted. 'I can just imagine the reaction if I'd asked.'

Anna nodded. 'Sean's idea of sharing chores was cooking a meal occasionally. But he left such chaos for me to clear up afterwards it wasn't worth it.'

'The more I hear about this man, the more I wonder what

made you move in with him in the first place,' said Ryder, shaking his head.

'Usual reason. I thought I was in love with him.'

'That obviously didn't last.'

She shrugged. 'He was hell-bent on making partnership for the firm of solicitors he worked for and put in gruellingly long hours, and I understood that because I have similar ambitions. Which means I work long hours too. Sean played hell when my free time didn't coincide with his.'

'He expected you to be on hand whenever he had a moment to spare for you, I suppose,' said Ryder scathingly.

'Exactly. Finally we had such a huge row about it I threatened to walk out. So Sean back-tracked pretty quickly. To smooth my ruffled feathers he suggested a weekend break at a luxury hotel. Unfortunately he forgot to book in time and there was no room at the inn he fancied, so we came down here to the cottage instead. After we got back we had a discussion which made it clear that Sean's idea of our future together was very different from mine, so I moved out.'

'Do you hear from him now?'

'Not so much lately. At first he rang me a lot with the same old sob story. He was unhappy and missed me terribly.' She shivered suddenly.

Ryder eyed her with concern. 'You're cold. Shall I put more logs on the fire or would you rather go to bed?'

She smiled guiltily. 'I think I would. This is so embarrassing.'

'What is?'

'Needing an early night just because I did some housework. Lord, I do so want to feel fit again!'

'You will soon enough, Anna.' Ryder got up and poked the fire. 'Stay there and keep warm. I'll be back in a minute.'

Anna kicked off her shoes and tucked her feet under her as she gazed into the dying embers, aware that in spite of weariness she felt a strong sense of well-being. Maybe it was the prospect of spending the night here again instead of alone at the cottage. Or because she and Ryder were friends again.

When Ryder came back he handed her a steaming mug of hot chocolate. 'I hope you still like this.'

Anna beamed at him in delight. 'Does a donkey like strawberries? Thanks, Ryder. How this takes me back. Mrs Carter used to make it for us in the winter holidays.' She rolled her eyes as she tasted her drink. 'Heavenly. You really know how to show a girl a good time, Mr Wyndham.'

'Not difficult where you're concerned, Anna.' He put another log on the fire, poured himself a finger of Scotch and sat down beside her. 'And before you hit me—which happened more than once in our youth—I meant that our wavelength is still operating enough for me to make an educated guess about your tastes.'

'In this instance you most certainly do,' she said, sipping.

'I put some cream in it. You're too thin, Anna.'

'Only recently. I lost weight when I was ill. But my appetite's perked up a bit since I arrived at the cottage.'

Ryder turned to look at her. 'Let's hope it stays that way when you get back to London. How soon do you go?'

Anna sipped her drink morosely. 'I'm due to start back in about a fortnight.'

'So you are staying a while longer?'

She nodded. 'At least by then Clare's cold should be better. If I go back earlier she threatens to take her germs elsewhere.'

'Where would she go?'

'She'd stay with Charlie, I suppose. Charlie Saunders, her ex-husband,' added Anna, turning to smile at Ryder. 'They get on a lot better now they're divorced. He's been looking after her while she's under the weather.'

'If the divorce is so amicable, what made them split up?' he asked curiously.

'Clare said it was the minutiae—her word—of daily living. He left damp towels on the bathroom floor; she left the cap off the toothpaste. That kind of thing. So now they spend social time together now and then and otherwise go their own ways. It's an odd relationship but it works.'

'It wouldn't for me,' said Ryder decisively. 'If I'm ever lucky enough to have a wife I'll make damn sure I hang on to her.'

'Easy,' said Anna, chuckling. 'Just put the towels back.'

'I already do that. Do you put the cap back on the toothpaste?'

'Every time.'

'No problem for you either, then.'

Anna clapped a hand over her mouth to hide a sudden yawn. 'Sorry. It must be the fire.'

'You're so tired you can't keep your eyes open.' Ryder took her empty mug away. 'Come on. I'll walk you upstairs.'

'Thanks, Ryder,' she said gratefully when they reached the blue room.

'Goodnight, Anna. Sleep well.' He opened the door for her and she smiled drowsily as she closed it.

Anna smiled again later when she found a hot-water bottle in the bed. Ryder Wyndham was not only better looking than any man had a right to be, he was thoughtful too. But there was steel behind the good looks and the charm, plus a sense of family pride inherited from several generations of Wyndhams. Edwina French had been a fool to try and trap him with the oldest trick in the book.

CHAPTER SIX

NEXT morning Anna scrambled out of bed in a tearing hurry, just in case Ryder took it into his head to bring her breakfast again. She washed her face and rubbed her teeth with a damp flannel, then pulled on the underwear she'd dried on the bathroom radiator and dressed at top speed. When she'd manhandled her hair into a loose braid she rummaged through her handbag and exclaimed in triumph when she found a tiny sample tube of moisturiser. She slapped it on, added a touch of lipstick and had just pulled on her shoes when Ryder knocked on the door.

'Come in,' she called.

'You're up!' He smiled, looking as rested as she felt. 'Did you sleep well?'

'Like a log.' She grinned. 'The hot-water bottle did the trick—nice touch, Ryder. Thanks!'

'All part of the Wyndham service. What would you like for breakfast?'

'Before I have breakfast I'll put that beef in the oven,' she said as they went downstairs.

'Then I'll do breakfast. What do you fancy?'

'Just toast made with Mrs Carter's fabulous bread, please.'

'How about bacon and eggs to go with it?'

'Not if we're having a big lunch.'

Ryder shook his head in disapproval as they went into the kitchen. 'You should eat more, Anna.'

'I'm doing that every day, little by little. I'm really quite a sensible female, Ryder! Now lead me to the pots and pans.'

It took a few false starts before Ryder found the type of pot Anna wanted for the roast. He grinned. 'I'm not very clued up in here.'

'No one would expect the Squire to know the way around his own kitchen,' she assured him.

'In my father's day—and in Eddy's—that was probably true,' he admitted as Anna switched on the cooker. 'I prefer a less feudal approach but I had to use a lot of persuasion to convince Martha I could cope without her at weekends.'

'Since you cope so well, you do the toast and coffee and leave me to rummage around in cupboards for what I want.'

'Much easier,' he agreed, laughing.

As Anna seared the joint of beef it struck her that her grandfather would have been delighted to see her on good terms with Ryder again. She felt rather good about it herself.

He looked up from the bread he was cutting as she put the meat in the oven. 'Is that my cue to make the toast, Anna?'

'Yes, sir!'

Anna was normally no fan of breakfast. It had taken strength of will to eat the poached egg the day before. But this morning she felt unusual enthusiasm for the meal.

'By the way, Ryder, I keep forgetting to ask. What happened to the dogs?'

'The last pair lived to quite a ripe old age. But they were Eddy's dogs. After he died they pined and refused to eat and in the end they had to be put down.' His face shadowed. 'That was a very bad time in my life. I couldn't face getting another dog for a while, but Dick Hammond says I can have my pick of his bitch's new litter. Want to come to Home Farm this morning to take a look?'

Her eyes lit up. 'Yes, please! I adored old Nell, Gramp's sheepdog, but when she died he said it wasn't fair to get another at his age.'

* * *

Anna checked on the beef after breakfast and announced that it had three hours or so to go before it was ready.

'In that case, let's get going,' said Ryder and cast a wry glance at her shoes. 'Not much good for farmyards, Anna.'

She smiled loftily. 'I keep boots in the car, ready for any footpath I take a fancy to when I'm driving around.'

'So you're still a country girl at heart,' he said with approval as they went outside. 'If you could find work in this area, would you live in Keeper's Cottage?'

'No. I've been used to city lights for a long time. Life alone at Keeper's Cottage is very attractive right now, but when I'm back to normal it could be a touch quiet—for a townie like me,' she added, making a face at him.

'I was used to city lights myself, but *I* adjusted,' he reminded her.

'Ah, but you said that deep down it was what you'd really wanted all along. To me this place means holidays and Gramp and running wild with you and Tom. Life alone here on a permanent basis would be very different.'

'I'm still here,' he pointed out.

'But there's no more running wild, Ryder.'

Anna unlocked the car and changed her shoes, then glanced up to see him outlined against the winter sky. As if Ryder wasn't handsome enough anyway, she thought, trying to look at him objectively. In the cold morning sunshine his hair shone like black silk and his eyes rivalled the clear blue sky. But, unlike his brother Dominic, the most attractive feature of Ryder's looks was his total disregard for them.

'Ready?' he said briskly. 'We'll drive. It's a bit far to hike to Home Farm.'

It was a nostalgia trip for Anna to tour the countryside she'd known so well when she was a child. 'There's our stream!' she said suddenly as they emerged from woodland. 'Remember when I fell in?'

'Which time?' he said dryly. 'You were always getting wet. And I always got the blame.'

'Gramp didn't blame you!'

'No, but my mother did. "A wonder that child doesn't get pneumonia!" was her constant cry.' Ryder slanted a wry smile at her. 'And one day you did. But I wasn't to blame that time.'

'You weren't to blame the other times either,' said Anna with justice. 'I was so determined to keep up I always forgot my legs were shorter than yours and Tom's when I tried to jump across.'

'To avoid another telling off I gave you a piggyback one day,' he reminded her. 'But we both fell in, and Tom jumped in after us, so we all got a row.'

'I know we can't have spent every day together,' said Anna, thinking about it, 'but looking back it seems as though we did.'

'I brought a school friend home for part of one holiday,' he reminded her.

'Toby Lonsdale! I'd forgotten about him.'

'He was quite smitten—kept banging on about you after we got back to school.'

'Really?' Anna batted her eyelashes. 'I wish I'd known!'

'He came to my famous party, so you must have met him again.'

'Yes. He danced with me.' She gave him an accusing look. 'You didn't, Ryder. I thought you were embarrassed because I didn't look right.'

'You couldn't have been more wrong. As host I just had to do my duty first, and when I came to look for you the bird had flown.' Ryder put a hand out to touch her knee. 'I wish I'd known you were unhappy that night, Anna.'

She shrugged. 'I was so young for my age. The other girls seemed light years older than me.' She jerked forward against the restraining seat belt as they turned into the heavily rutted lane to Home Farm.

'Hold tight,' he warned.

Anna held on to the door handle as the Land Rover bucked

its way down the lane and came to a halt at the Home Farm stables. A couple of sheepdogs and a big golden retriever came barking with Dick Hammond in pursuit, grinning in welcome.

'Good morning, both—quiet, you lot! How are you then, Anna? I heard you'd been ill. We thought you looked very pale at the funeral.'

Anna smiled as Ryder lifted her down. 'I'm much better now. Thank you for coming that day.' She held out her hand, palm down, for the dogs to sniff.

'It was a good do. Hector would have enjoyed it.'

'So where are these pups, Dick?' asked Ryder, fondling Nelson's noble head. 'Do I get a discount if I buy two?'

'The Squire likes his little jokes,' Dick told Anna, rolling his eyes. 'Come in the house then. I've got them in the scullery so it's easy for Jen to keep an eye on them. You stay out there with the others, Nelson. You did your part long ago.'

Anna was about to kick off her boots at the kitchen door, but Jennifer Hammond came hurrying to stop her.

'You keep them on, dear. I'd rather a bit of mud on my kitchen floor than have you poorly again.'

'Thanks, Mrs Hammond.' Anna sniffed appreciatively. 'Lovely smell. I hope we're not holding you up.'

'Not a bit. I'll have coffee ready by the time you've seen the pups.' She smiled at Ryder. 'How are you this morning?'

'All the better for seeing you, Jen.' He kissed her cheek. 'Right then, Dick. Let's see the merchandise.'

They went through into a scullery almost as big as the one up at the Manor. At the far end a golden retriever bitch lay in state in a blanket-lined box with six small squirming bundles fighting for pole position against her.

'This is Lady Hamilton,' Dick told Anna, 'but we just call her Lady.'

'And what a lady you are,' crooned Anna, dropping to her knees. 'Will she let me stroke her, Mr Hammond?'

'Of course, but keep away from her pups.'

Anna kept a discreet distance from them as she stroked the shining golden head, telling Lady how clever she was to produce such handsome babies.

Ryder watched in amusement. 'I'd like two dogs for preference, Dick.'

'Right. Come back in a day or two when they're bigger and take your pick. They'll be ready to go in six weeks or so.'

Half an hour later, after estate talk over coffee and Jennifer's scones, Anna and Ryder got back in the car.

'Do you want another drive,' said Ryder as they headed up the lane, 'or shall we make for home?'

'I'd better check on the roast,' said Anna. She looked up at the sky. 'And it looks like rain, anyway.'

'Home it is, then.'

As they reached the back courtyard of the Manor the heavens opened. Ryder stuck Anna's shoes in the pockets of his jacket and got out to sprint round the car. He scooped her from her seat, then raced with her into the back entry and set her on her feet outside the kitchen door, panting.

'You said I was too thin,' she reminded him.

'The speed did the damage,' he said breathlessly as they went inside. He combed fingers through wet curls spiralling round his head like parcel ribbon and handed her the shoes. 'There you are, Cinderella.'

Anna put them on and hurried inside, anxious about the roast. She slung her sheepskin on the back of a chair, then took oven gloves from a hook and removed the heavy red pot from the oven. She took the lid off with care, releasing mouth-watering scents they sniffed in unison.

'Smells good,' said Ryder, impressed.

Anna searched through the kitchen drawers nearest the stove until she found a meat thermometer. She plunged the spike into the meat and watched as the needle rose. 'Nearly there. I'll put it back for a bit while I do the vegetables.'

'Sit down for a while first.'

Anna returned the pot to the oven, then spun round, glaring. 'Ryder, I don't *need* to sit down. Where does Mrs Carter keep the potatoes?'

He glowered back. 'Am I at least allowed to fetch them for you?'

'OK. Sorry, I didn't mean to snap your head off.'

'I'll forgive you this once—which is more than you did for me,' he added significantly.

'*Slightly* different crime, Ryder Wyndham. Now, can I have the potatoes, please, and anything else you can find?'

The beef was tender, the roast potatoes crunchy, the cabbage crisp and green and the rich gravy perfect, according to Ryder.

'Thank goodness,' said Anna, as she began on her own meal. 'I don't get much practice at this kind of thing and the trick is to get everything ready and hot at once. Normally I only cook this kind of food at home with Dad when Gramp's there. *Was* there,' she added with a sigh, and smiled valiantly. 'He was very partial to roast beef, but he liked Yorkshire pudding with it. I wasn't brave enough to try that today.'

'There's always next time,' said Ryder. 'Now you have Keeper's Cottage as a base we could do this now and again.'

'To save you fending for yourself?'

'No, to give me the pleasure of your company.'

Anna smiled into the gleaming blue eyes. 'You know exactly which buttons to push, Ryder Wyndham.'

He nodded smugly. 'As I've said before, whatever works!'

She sighed. 'I won't be able to come very often. I'm usually so tired by Friday night, I spend Saturday catching up on sleep.'

'What kind of life is that?' he demanded. 'Can't you find something less exhausting?'

'Not if I want partnership in the firm, Ryder.'

'Is that really all you want out of life?'

'It's certainly my ambition. I enjoy my job a whole lot more than sharing my life with a man, if that's what you mean,' she informed him tartly. 'That turned out to be a big fat mistake.'

'Only because it was the wrong man, Anna.'

'Possibly. But it's put me off trying it again any time soon. Finish off the potatoes.'

Ryder noted the change in subject, but obeyed with alacrity. 'You're a good cook, Anna.'

'I wouldn't say that. Anyone can put a joint of meat in the oven—even you.' She smiled sweetly. 'Now you've seen how easy it is you can do this for yourself every week.'

Ryder was so obviously unused to clearing away after a meal that Anna sent him off to read the Sunday papers and got busy herself. It took a while before she felt that everything was tidy enough to please Mrs Carter, but at last she called Ryder back in. 'Right then, everything's shipshape, so are you going to keep your promise?'

He nodded. 'We'll start hunting for Violet and Ned right away. Follow me. I think it's stopped raining.'

The estate office was in the stable block. It was scrupulously tidy, with a leather-topped table as a desk and ledgers ranged along shelves in order of the dates printed on the spines.

'What's in the filing cabinets?' asked Anna, impressed.

'The more modern stuff. The retired estate manager was the original Luddite. He wouldn't have anything to do with electronics, but since I took over I've spent a lot of weekends computerising the records. When I'm completely up-to-date life should be easier—and I'll know a whole lot more about the estate.'

'You've got your work cut out,' she said with respect.

Ryder went behind the desk to look along the shelves and took down three of the ledgers. '1914 to 16 and 1917 to 18 should do it. That black ledger at the end contains the records of births, deaths and marriages, which is probably the best one for you. If our Violet was married to Ned, you could start from the end of the last century about the time she was born.'

'Unless Ned took her there as a bride.'

'True. But we have to start somewhere. Let's take these back to the kitchen.'

It took a long time, with both of them glued to different books at the table in the warm kitchen, before they made any headway. At last Ryder looked up in triumph. 'A new assistant gamekeeper was hired in 1910, name of Albert Hodge, wife Winifred, sons Stanley and George, daughter Violet. To be housed in Keeper's Cottage.'

'Brilliant! Now we just have to find Ned,' said Anna, delighted. 'I'll look in the weddings.'

After a search she managed to find Violet Hodge's wedding, but the date was April 1918 and the bridegroom was listed as James Bloxham, carpenter.

Ryder's eyebrows rose as he looked over her shoulder. 'A month after Ned's last letter. She didn't wait long.'

Anna stared at the entry in silence for a while. 'Would James Bloxham have worked on the estate?'

'A whole family of Bloxhams did once. Why?'

'To see if his name crops up afterwards somewhere.' Anna leafed quickly through the births section, then stopped, marking an entry with her fingernail. 'There. Francis James Bloxham, born August 1918 to Violet and James Bloxham.' She bit her lip. 'That's why she didn't wait. She was expecting a child, Ned's probably.'

Ryder looked down his nose. 'In that case she must have had a fling with James as well if he was willing to marry her.'

'People in that era in this kind of close community didn't have flings,' said Anna impatiently. 'According to Ned's letters Violet was beautiful so maybe James was willing to take her on even though she was carrying another man's child.'

'Brave man if he was. I couldn't do it,' said Ryder flatly, and then shut the books as Anna shivered. 'Enough for today,' he said firmly.

'May I make some tea?' she asked.

'Of course. No need to ask.'

'I was brought up to be polite!'

'You always were. Tom, too. My mother used to remark on

it, hoping your manners would rub off on Dominic. He was a little savage.'

'But adorable with it,' said Anna, filling the kettle.

'Which was why he was such a little savage. Arriving so long after me, he was utterly ruined by my parents. Mother, in particular, was besotted with him.'

'Were you jealous?'

'No. I was besotted with him too—until he told me you were going to marry him.'

'For heaven's sake don't start all that again!' She eyed him objectively. 'You and Dominic are very alike, physically, but Edward was quite different.'

'He had Mother's fair hair and delicate build, but he was tough as whipcord just the same. Eddy was a good man. I miss him.' Ryder squared his shoulders and took a large tin from one of the overhead cupboards. 'Martha always leaves me a cake. Want some?'

'No room, thanks. And if anyone's ruined, it's you. Mrs Carter spoils you rotten,' said Anna. 'How can you even think of cake after that lunch?'

'Strictly between you and me, I'm not keen on cake at any time, but I eat a slice now and then to please Martha. Most of it goes to her cleaning crew and the garden staff during tea breaks.'

Anna sat at the table, frowning, as she sipped her tea. 'Where else can we look for Ned?'

'The church records?'

Her eyes lit up. 'Of course. I'll pop over there tomorrow and ask the vicar if I can take a look.'

'I've been thinking, Anna,' said Ryder, a note in his voice which won him a wary look. 'I think you'd better stay here until Brian's made the cottage burglar-proof.'

'I can't do that,' she protested.

'Be sensible, Anna. Do you really want to go back before the window's mended and the alarm system installed?'

'No,' she said after a moment's thought, 'I suppose not.'

'End of argument, then,' he said briskly.

'But if I'm going to stay for a day or so I'll need my things. I'd better drive over now.'

'Not on your own, Anna. I'll take you.'

She stared at him, exasperated. 'You may be surprised to know, Ryder Wyndham, that I managed my life perfectly well on my own for years without your help.'

He nodded impatiently. 'Don't be difficult, Anna. I just want to make sure everything's secure at the cottage for the night.'

Anna was secretly very glad of Ryder's company as she hurried up her garden path in the dark later, even though she'd left the lights on the night before.

'Leave them on tonight too,' he instructed. 'I'll look round outside while you pack.'

Even with Ryder close at hand Anna felt on edge as she filled her suitcase. Once the house was secure again she would be fine, she assured herself. And, in any case, she wouldn't be here all that long. Soon she had to go back to the real world. Ryder was waiting at the foot of the stairs as she went down with her suitcase.

'You man hasn't returned to the scene of his crime as far as I can see,' he told her.

'Good. I'm packed and ready.' She eyed him uncertainly. 'Should I bring anything with me for supper?'

'No. We'll dine on leftover roast beef, so let's lock up everything we can lock and get back to the Manor.' He smiled, looking more like the Ryder of old. 'I'll even make the sandwiches if you ask me nicely.'

'You're an absolute star, Ryder Wyndham,' she mocked. 'Edwina must be mad as hell that you sent her packing.'

'Why?'

'Because, apart from a certain aloofness which is only natural to a man in your exalted circumstances—'

'Aloof? I'm the soul of friendliness,' he protested.

'Not all the time, as far as I'm concerned,' she reminded him tartly. 'But in general you're kind, thoughtful—'

'For God's sake,' he said in disgust. 'If you must sling adjectives around, how about irresistible and sexy?'

'Those too,' she assured him and grinned as he eyed her balefully.

'I was joking, Anna!'

'I wasn't.' She wagged a finger at him. 'I know perfectly well that at one time you had a conveyor belt of girlfriends who agreed with me.'

He shrugged. 'My money was the big attraction.'

'Rubbish!'

Ryder closed the front door and made sure it was secure, then took her bag down to the Land Rover. He drove back to the Manor with such speed and panache Anna was thankful the vehicle was a four-wheel drive rather than one of the high-powered sports cars that Ryder kept locked away most of the time these days.

'Right,' she said breathlessly as he helped her down in the back courtyard. 'I'll just go and unpack my case.'

'While you're upstairs I'll slice some roast beef. Sandwiches,' he added, grinning down at her, 'are *de rigueur* here for Sunday supper.'

'Sounds good to me,' she said cheerfully. 'I'll just go up to the blue room, then.'

'I'll carry your bag for you.'

Anna was glad to let him to do so. She was perfectly capable of carrying the bag herself, but walking upstairs alone past the portraits of former Wyndhams intensified her feeling of intrusion. She couldn't rid herself of the feeling that they looked down their Wyndham noses in disdain at the gamekeeper's brat who had no right to be here in this beautiful house. Which was utterly stupid, she told herself irritably, when Ryder left her alone. Class distinction was supposed to be a thing of the past. She was a highly qualified accountant in a firm where the other employees at her level were all men, most of whom looked on her as an equal. When they were young she'd thought of Ryder as her equal too, and would probably still think the same way if it hadn't been for the famous party where she'd discovered that some people, like Anna Morton, were considered less equal than others. She shrugged the thought away as she unpacked and went downstairs to help Ryder with supper.

'When are you going to tell your father about the break-in?' asked Ryder later, as they sat down to eat.

'Next time I see him. No point in worrying him. And by then I'll be due back in London, anyway.'

Ryder shot her a gleaming look. 'You know, Anna, this is our third evening together and so far we haven't clashed swords even once.'

'No reason why we should,' she said, unruffled. 'With one notable exception, we never quarrelled in the past.'

'True. What do you want to do after supper? Are you a television fanatic?'

Anna shook her head. 'I'll keep that for when I'm on my own. Tell me about Hannah.'

Ryder smiled indulgently. 'She's a charmer. Dominic's a lucky man.'

'You like her, then.'

He nodded. 'So much that to make up for her disappointment about the wedding I'm giving a ball to introduce Dominic's fiancée to the locals instead. It's time I repaid some of my social obligations. This would be a good way to do it all at once.'

'I suppose you're inviting half the county?'

'Not that many. Hannah's family are flying over for the occasion and I'll invite various relatives of mine to meet them. Old friends like the Mortons are on the list too,' he added.

Anna stared at him in surprise. 'You're inviting *us*?'

'Of course. Dominic said to make sure I asked you all personally before the invitations go out.' Ryder smiled. 'Will you come, Anna?'

'I wouldn't miss it for the world,' she assured him.

He raised a wry eyebrow. 'If the invitation had been sent to you a couple of weeks ago, before we declared a truce, would you have refused?'

Anna thought it over. 'Probably not, if Dad and Tom were invited too.'

'And Hector. I gave him advance warning about his invitation when I asked his advice on the best place to put the marquee and so on—what's the matter?'

Anna gazed at him, wide-eyed. 'You invited *Gramp*?'

'Of course I did. He told me he was too old for such things, but he was very pleased.'

'So am I!' She jumped up and kissed Ryder with such gratitude that his arms closed round her in reflex action for a moment before she dodged away, flushing.

'Sorry.'

'I'm not,' he assured her, eyes gleaming. 'Feel free to do that any time you like.'

Anna sat down hurriedly. 'I'm not the demonstrative type, Ryder.'

He eyed her with interest. 'Not even with the ex-lover?'

Her colour rose again. 'I'd rather not talk about that,' she said stiffly.

'Is it that painful?' he asked, refilling her wineglass.

'Any relationship that ends so acrimoniously is painful to look back on, I suppose.' She hesitated for a moment. 'If you really want to know—'

'Which I do,' he said promptly.

'It all came to a head when Sean achieved partnership in his firm soon after we came down here for the weekend.' Anna downed some of her wine. 'I wasn't getting any younger, he pointed out. It was the perfect time to buy a house and start a family.'

'What about your career?'

Anna's mouth clenched. 'I was to give it up once I started having children. Sean doesn't approve of women who want it all. It would have meant goodbye to any partnership.'

Ryder sat back in his chair, fascinated. 'The idea obviously didn't appeal to you.'

'It appalled me,' she said with a shudder. 'A woman needs to love a man very deeply to change her life to that extent for him. I realised that my feelings for Sean were nothing remotely like that, so I left and moved in with Clare. But, to fill the sudden blank in my life, I worked longer hours than usual, went back to the office too soon after flu and went down with pneumonia. One way and another, I desperately needed this time here to get body and soul back in working order again.' Her eyes kindled. 'The last thing I expected was a burglary to add to my joys.'

'You can rest easy while you're here at the Manor—' Ryder got up with a word of apology as the phone rang and began a conversation which consisted on his part of reiterated assurances that he would manage very well, that he had enough food in the house to feed a small army and on no account was Martha to come back until she was better.

'Is Mrs Carter ill?' asked Anna, beginning to clear the table.

'A very heavy cold by the sound of it.' Ryder smiled affectionately. 'Martha's afraid I won't feed myself properly.'

'More likely she thinks the Squire shouldn't have to fend for himself!'

'Whereas the "Squire" can manage very efficiently on his own, and did so for years before acceding to his present eminence,' said Ryder cuttingly.

'So you did.' Anna gave him a rueful smile. 'Sorry.'

His eyes softened. 'You never miss a chance, do you?'

'I know a way to make up,' she offered.

'Another kiss?'

'Something better than that. I suggest I earn my keep by organising the meals while I'm here.'

'Disappointing,' he said lightly, 'but an offer I won't refuse. There are one or two other things you could help me with too. I'm tied up with Dick Hammond tomorrow, but if you could organise coffee for the mid-morning break I'd be grateful. Carol,

Alison and the others know the drill, but perhaps you'd provide the garden crew with theirs.'

'Certainly. But won't they think it odd that I'm doing it?'

Ryder's face took on what Anna secretly thought of as his Lord of the Manor look. 'Why should they think it odd? If anyone has the nerve to ask, tell them you're staying here while the repairs are done on your cottage.'

'Right,' she said briskly, once the kitchen was immaculate again. 'What else can I do to help?'

'Nothing for the time being, so unless you want a really early night I suggest we read the Sunday papers in the morning room. I'll light the fire.'

'Sounds good to me,' said Anna. 'But in the morning, once I've done the coffee break, I'll ring the vicar and see if he can help me with some research.' She smiled. 'I feel proprietorial about Violet because she lived in Keeper's Cottage.'

'I'm curious about the mysterious Ned too,' admitted Ryder as they crossed the hall.

'By his handwriting and his polished syntax, he was obviously well-educated,' said Anna. 'I bet Violet was madly in love with him.'

'Why are you so certain?' asked Ryder, putting a match to the fire.

'Ned really loved her by the tone of his letters. How could she not be in love with him?'

'I'm no expert on the subject, Anna,' he said, shrugging. 'I've enjoyed the company of several women in my time, but, unlike you, I've never been in love.'

'I haven't either. I thought I was with Sean but I was mistaken. Not,' she added grimly, 'a mistake I'll repeat.'

Ryder stared into the fire. 'I'd like to think that I'll find someone to share my life one day. Feudal as it may sound, I'd like an heir. That's why I never hesitated about marrying Edwina when she said she was pregnant. I certainly wasn't in love with her the way Dominic is with Hannah.'

'Does she feel the same about him?'

'Lord, yes. She thinks the sun shines out of his big blue eyes!'

They were both silent for a while after that, leafing through the papers as the fire crackled into life.

'By the way,' said Ryder eventually. 'You'd better give me your key. I'll get it over to Brian first thing before I meet Dick.'

'I can do that,' she said instantly.

'Better if I do it. I'll emphasise that the work is urgent—'

'And because you're the Squire Brian will get it done at top speed.'

'Exactly.'

'There's the feudal bit again!'

'Possibly, but it works, Anna. Would you pass me the financial section?'

The rest of the evening was so amicable and relaxed that Anna was sorry when Ryder got up as the clock struck eleven.

'I'll just make the fire safe before we go up.'

'What time will Mrs Carter's cleaning crew arrive?' asked Anna as they went upstairs together later.

'Nine. Bob Godfrey and his gardeners start at eight.'

'Mr Godfrey's still head gardener?' she exclaimed. 'He can't be much younger than Gramp.'

'He can't bear the thought of retiring, so I'm letting him carry on until he's had enough,' said Ryder, and then caught her by the elbow as she stumbled over the top stair. 'Steady,' he said lightly, the fleeting contact causing sudden tension between them as he walked with her to the blue room. He opened the door and gave her a look which made her uneasy.

'Do you have everything you need, Anna?'

'Yes, thank you. Goodnight, Ryder.' She smiled briefly and went inside, closing the door very quietly behind her. As she got ready for the night Anna hoped Brian James was a fast worker. It wouldn't do to stay here at the Manor any longer than strictly necessary.

CHAPTER SEVEN

NEXT morning Ryder was gone by the time Anna went down to the kitchen, with a note to say he'd be out most of the day, including lunch, but could be reached by phone if she needed him.

After a hasty cup of coffee Anna barely had time to make the kitchen inspection perfect before the cleaners arrived for their Monday morning shift. Carol, Alison, Peggy and Jean were friendly women in their forties who had all known Hector Morton well. They introduced themselves to Anna, expressed their condolences, commiserated with her about the burglary and exclaimed over the fact that Mrs Carter was too poorly to report for work.

'Never known her to be ill before,' declared Carol, a tall, well-built woman with a pleasant smile. 'I'll be foreman today then, Miss Morton. Don't worry, we've been doing this for years so we know the drill. Did Squire tell you the gardeners get coffee at ten-thirty? We'll see to them when we make ours, if you like.'

'Thank you. That would be an enormous help. Mrs Carter left a cake in the blue tin as usual.' Anna smiled gratefully. 'I'll be in the office, doing some work for Mr Wyndham.'

Ryder was so organised that Anna had no trouble in finding out where he'd paused in his task of computerising the estate records. She booted up his computer, familiarised herself with his files, then got to work. She was soon so immersed that she

looked up in surprise when Alison arrived with a cup of coffee
and announced that it was ten-thirty and time for a break.

'That's very sweet of you,' she said, embarrassed, 'but I didn't
mean to add to your labours by waiting on me.'

'No trouble,' said the woman cheerfully. 'Bob Godfrey and
his boys have all had theirs. Carol said to let you know that we
all finish at one, garden crew included at this time of year.'

To Anna's embarrassment, Carol came to fetch her before the
cleaners left and took her on a tour of the ground floor rooms to
inspect the morning's work. 'So you can tell Squire we're pulling
our weight while Mrs Carter's away,' she said with a chuckle.

'It all looks beautiful,' Anna assured her.

'By the way, Bob Godfrey left you some fresh vegetables,'
said Carol. 'I put them with the others in the scullery.'

After the women had gone Anna checked to see how much
roast beef was left and decided Ryder could make do with
cottage pie for once in his life. After a swift sandwich, she rang
the Reverend Oliver Jessop, reiterated her appreciation of the
beautiful funeral service for her grandfather and asked if he
could spare a few moments to talk to her that afternoon.

'I was hoping you might be able to help me trace a man,
possibly local, who died in the First World War.'

'How intriguing, Anna,' said the vicar with enthusiasm. 'My
wife is the best one to consult on that subject. Come for tea about
three this afternoon. We'll be only too delighted to help if we
can.'

'You're sure you're not busy?'

'Not today. I take a breather on Monday before tackling the
rest of the week.'

Anna took time to prepare dinner before going off to tea at
the vicarage. A little more at home in the kitchen by this time,
she put potatoes on to boil while she chopped and fried onions
and minced the beef and, with the help of leftover gravy from
the roast, she felt fairly satisfied with the results. She put the pie
on a marble slab in the scullery, ready to heat up later, but

washed her hands at the kitchen sink rather than go back up to her room now she was alone in the house.

Anna set out early for the village to allow time to linger for a few minutes at Hector's grave before making for the vicarage. Oliver Jessop, a tall thin man with a magnificent head of grey hair, opened the door in smiling welcome as the church clock struck three.

'Punctual to the minute, Anna. How are you, my dear?' He called down the hall to his wife as he led Anna into a comfortable study with rubbed leather furniture and a blazing fire.

Helen Jessop, also grey-haired and thin, followed them in with a tea tray, smiling warmly at the visitor. 'Anna, this is such a nice surprise. My goodness, you look so much better than when we saw you last. Ghastly thing, pneumonia. Have a bit of my shortbread.' She filled cups and handed one to Anna. 'But what's all this about a burglary, dear? Oliver heard about it after morning service yesterday and went straight over to Keeper's to see you, but you were out.'

Anna gave them a brief account of the break-in. 'I'm not so concerned about the television and so on, but I think the thief must have taken Gramp's gold hunter. Ryder Wyndham helped me search the entire cottage for it, but no luck—this was the only thing we found.' She produced the box. 'Can you shed some light on the letters in it? We traced Violet in the estate records yesterday, but Ned remains a mystery.'

Oliver Jessop took the box with reverence and moved closer to his wife so they could read them together.

'Oh, *dear*,' said Mrs Jessop with a sigh when they'd finished the last one. 'How very sad.'

Anna nodded soberly. 'Are there some records I could look at to search for Ned?'

Oliver Jessop hesitated, exchanged a look with his wife, then patted Anna's hand. 'Come into the church first.'

Surprised, Anna crossed the graveyard with the Jessops and followed them down the central aisle in the church. The vicar silently pointed to the wall near the pulpit, where a faded flag hung above a marble plaque.

> *Captain Edward Francis Ryder Wyndham, MC*
> *Royal Welsh Fusiliers*
> *Killed in Action, March 18th, 1918*
> *Beloved son and brother.*

Anna stared at the plaque, transfixed. 'But surely there was more than one Edward from the village in the army?' she said at last.

Mrs Jessop nodded briskly. 'There was indeed. Come back to the house and we'll show you the list.'

But when Anna pored over the records she found that of the local young men who went for a soldier, those christened Edward were either killed earlier than Captain Wyndham or survived and came home.

'If the Captain really is the Ned of the letters, Ryder should be able to tell you more about him,' said Oliver Jessop, looking a little uncomfortable.

'I'll report to him later on my findings,' said Anna. 'Thank you both so much for your help.'

Anna drove back to the Manor in a state of suppressed excitement, wishing Ryder were home so she could give him the news straight away. Instead she received a phone call on her mobile from her father and, as expected, he hit the roof when she told him about the burglary.

'Why in God's name didn't you ring me?' he demanded wrathfully.

'I was going to tell you about it when you came the next day, but you couldn't make it so it seemed pointless to worry you before I saw you again, Dad.'

'Pointless!' said her father explosively. 'I hope to God you weren't there at the time.'

'I was out, Dad. It was literally daylight robbery.'

'I suppose I should be thankful for that, at least!'

'I made a list of what was taken—'

'To hell with any list,' he snapped. 'I just hate to think of you coping with something like that on your own.'

'Actually I didn't. I rang Ryder.'

'Did you indeed?' said her father, surprised. 'I thought he wasn't your favourite person these days.'

'We've sorted that out now. He told me to ring him if I ever needed anything. I was totally freaked out by the burglary and he was on the spot so I took him up on the offer. He's been very helpful.'

'Knowing Ryder, I'm sure he has. I'm very grateful to him. Was there any damage to the cottage?'

Anna reassured her anxious father that there'd been nothing serious and told him what had been taken, as far as she could tell. 'But I couldn't find Gramp's gold hunter, Dad. That must have gone with the rest.'

'No, darling,' said Dr Morton quickly. 'Father gave it to me last time I saw him.'

'Oh, thank goodness! That's such a relief.' Anna went on to tell him about Ryder's gift of a new television and the work that was being done to make the cottage secure, but none of it diverted her father from his main worry.

'I think you should get in the car right now and drive straight here,' he said emphatically. 'I'd come myself this minute, but—'

'No way, Dad. I knew you'd say that, which is why I didn't tell you before. You've got evening surgery to get through. And, although I'm much better, I'm not up to a long drive today. Oh, and I forgot—' Anna told him about the letters and the research she'd been doing with Ryder and the Jessops. She braced herself. 'And there's no need to worry about me because Ryder insists I stay at the Manor until the repairs are done on the cottage.'

'Really?' said her father, sounding astonished. 'That's extraordinarily good of him. Make sure you thank him on my behalf—and ask him to send me the bill for the work.'

'Will do, Dad.'

The rest of the conversation centred on Anna's convalescence and how soon she expected to return to her job.

'Be very careful this time, Anna. Remember what happened when you went back too soon after your flu,' her father reminded her. 'I'll drive down the weekend after next when I'm not working and make sure you're as well as you say.'

'Yes, Doctor,' she said meekly. 'The cottage will be ready by then, so stay the night if you like.'

'Not this time, pet. I've been asked out to lunch that Sunday. Must dash. Take care, I'll ring again tomorrow.'

When she disconnected Anna went into the office to look through the ledger which gave details of births and deaths. After a search she found the entries she was looking for, gazed at them in silence, then put the ledger away and went back to the kitchen, her mood sober as she took carrots and parsnips from the fresh supplies of vegetables. She peeled them ready to cook later, then laid the kitchen table, decided it was too late for more work on the computer and finally plucked up enough courage to go upstairs alone once she'd switched on all the lights. She hurried past the portraits of former Wyndhams, feeling like an interloper as usual. Rubbish, she thought with sudden impatience and hurried along the landing to her room to take a shower. She wrapped herself in a towel afterwards and looked through her choice of clothes, wishing she'd packed more, then jumped yards when a loud knock on the door frightened the life out of her.

'Anna,' called Ryder, 'I'm back.'

She opened the door cautiously. 'You're early!'

Ryder swallowed as he eyed the expanse of flushed skin left bare by the towel she was clutching and pulled himself together hurriedly. 'I tend to get home by this time for Martha's sake. I rang to warn you I was on my way,' he added.

'I was in the shower.'

'I need one too,' he said, clearing his throat. Preferably cold. 'I pitched in with some physical work on the boundary fencing today and my muscles will complain if I hang about.' God, he was babbling. 'How was your day?'

'Eventful,' she told him. 'I'll tell you about it over dinner.'

'Give me half an hour and I'll be with you. I've opened a bottle of wine,' he said over his shoulder. 'Will the meal hang about if we have a drink first?'

'It certainly will. But don't get your hopes up. It's not cordon bleu stuff, Ryder.'

'You cook it, I'll eat it,' he assured her and took off for his room like a man running for cover.

She'd been just as embarrassed, Anna thought resentfully, cheeks burning. She dressed hurriedly, slapped some make-up on and went down to the kitchen to switch on the oven. To her relief it was more than half an hour before Ryder put in an appearance. When he finally joined her, looking comfortable in faded jeans and a cricket sweater, his hair still damp, he sniffed the air with anticipation as he poured wine.

'Something smells wonderful. If it's not ready yet let's go into the morning room to drink this.'

Anna shook her head, smiling. 'The cook would rather stay here to make sure the dinner doesn't burn.'

'You're the boss.' Ryder held out a chair for her. 'I wasn't sure about the menu so I took a chance and opened some heavy duty red.'

'Perfect,' said Anna, tasting it. 'Any news of Mrs Carter?'

He nodded. 'I called in on her on the way home and she's at the messy sneezing stage. I told her I would be extremely displeased if she came back before she felt better, but the risk of giving us her germs persuaded her in the end.'

'Poor dear. Should I go and see her tomorrow?'

'She wouldn't let you through the door if you did. Give her a ring instead.' Ryder leaned back in his chair, trying to forget the insecure towel she'd been wearing earlier. 'I like that jersey. The colour matches your hair, Anna.'

'I didn't pack enough clothes to ring the changes very much. I wasn't thinking too clearly when I left London.'

'Understandable. You'd been ill and you were on your way to Hector's funeral—not the best of combinations for travelling.' Ryder sniffed the air again hopefully. 'I hate to rush the chef, but will dinner be ready soon? I'm starving.'

'I'll see what I can do, Squire.' Anna got up to take the dinner plates from the warming oven. 'It's pretty basic stuff,' she warned him as she put one down in front of him.

'If it tastes the way it smells I shan't complain!'

The cheese-topped potato crust on the cottage pie was a crisp golden brown Anna was rather pleased with as she set it on the table. She decanted glazed roast parsnips and carrots into a serving dish to accompany the pie and sat down. 'I hope you like this kind of thing, Ryder.'

He helped himself to a large portion and rolled his eyes as he tasted it. 'Fantastic! How could I not like it? Was this one of Hector's recipes?'

'No. Charlie Saunders showed me how to do it. He's a terrific cook.'

'So are you, Anna. This is even better than Martha's. What magic did you perform on these vegetables?'

'Just a tiny smear of honey and mustard.' Her eyes gleamed. 'I must say I'm still surprised that you eat ordinary fare like cottage pie at Wyndham Manor.'

'You harbour a lot of misconceptions about life here, Anna,' he retorted. 'Though, after today, you know rather more about what goes on.'

'I certainly do. Carol and her crew did a wonderful job on the ground floor reception rooms. They also catered for Mr Godfrey and his lads when they stopped for a break, and even brought coffee to the office for me.'

Ryder frowned. 'What were you doing in there? Searching for Ned?'

Anna shook her head, flushing. 'I transferred a few more files to your computer and stored them on disk with the ones you'd already done. I couldn't hang around with nothing to do.' Her chin lifted. 'But I won't do it again if you object.'

'Feel free to beat my records into shape any time you like,' said Ryder warmly, 'as long as you don't tire yourself. I'd hate to face your father if you suffered a relapse on my account.'

'Of course I won't,' she said impatiently. 'Talking of Dad, he rang me this afternoon and I finally told him about the break-in. He went up like a rocket, as expected, and ordered me home, but he calmed down a lot when I told him you'd come riding to my rescue.'

'Does he know you're staying here?'

'Yes.'

'And is he happy about it?'

'Of course he is. Ryder Wyndham can do no wrong as far as my family's concerned.' She gave him an evil little smile. 'Don't worry. I didn't shatter their illusions.'

He frowned. 'You didn't tell them about my visit to your flat?'

'No, though my subsequent coolness towards you puzzled Dad and Tom quite a bit!'

He reached over to refill her glass. 'Brian rang me earlier to say the window is back in and the ledge and brickwork replaced, but there's some sealing and painting to do. The locks are fitted, but he's had to order the alarm. He'll install it the moment it arrives, he assured me.' Ryder raised his glass to her. 'So my houseguest can't run away just yet.'

'In that case, dinner will be something from the freezer tomorrow night.'

'We could always go down to the Red Lion.'

Heaven forbid. 'No, thank you, Ryder. I'll manage something, I promise.'

'Did you have time to contact the vicar?'

'I certainly did. Once I've cleared away and made coffee, I'll make my report. No,' she added, as he got up to help, 'I'll be quicker on my own.'

'Then I'll light the fire in the morning room while I'm waiting.'

Anna made short work of clearing away and stacking the dishwasher, then made a pot of coffee and went across the hall to the morning room.

'Come in,' said Ryder, taking the tray. 'You sit, I'll pour.' He handed her one of the tall mugs she'd chosen in preference to the best china and then sat down beside her with his own, stretching out his legs with a sigh of pleasure. 'After a hard, physical kind of day it's good just to sit and relax, Anna. The women in my former life were all party animals, Edwina included.'

'If our spare time coincided, Sean was too.' She smiled demurely at Ryder. 'Whereas you, Squire, are surprisingly restful company.'

'Likewise, Miss Morton,' he retorted. 'Now, tell me what you found out at the vicarage.'

'In the church, actually,' she said warily, wondering how he'd take the news. On impulse she took his hand as she described the tablet in the church. 'There's no proof, of course, and the Jessops were a bit embarrassed when they showed it to me, but it seems likely that your great-uncle Edward Wyndham was Violet's Ned.'

'Good God!' Ryder stared down at her, arrested. 'Are you sure?'

'I looked through the records and the dates fit. And Violet used one of his names for her son. At this point it struck me that you might have an elderly relative by the name of Francis Bloxham still around somewhere, so I did some more digging in the births, marriages and deaths when I got back.' She sighed. 'I found that, along with several others in the district, Violet and her baby son died in the flu epidemic at the end of the war.'

His hand tightened on hers. 'What a tragic little tale,' he said very quietly.

They sat together in silence for a while, staring into the flames.

'It's a story with a moral, Anna,' said Ryder at last. 'Life's too short to waste a second of it.'

'True.' She shivered a little. 'So what shall I fill my seconds with tomorrow? The upper floor gets the treatment in the morning, apparently, so I'll lie low in the office again out of the way. Shall I carry on with the records or is there something else you'd prefer me to do?'

'You don't have to do anything, Anna. Why not go out for the day?'

'No,' she said firmly. 'I prefer to make myself useful.'

'In that case, perhaps you'd like to look at my arrangements for the ball. It's only six weeks away so you could check on the suppliers to make sure everything's going to plan.'

'Right. How far have you got?'

'The invitations arrived last week. I've sent the ones by airmail, but you could get the others off for me. I've also ordered the marquee, but I was very specific in my require-ments, as you'll see from the file, so you could check that they're sending the right one. I've booked the caterers and the band, also accommodation at the Red Lion and Over Court Hotel for some people. The Breckenridge party, along with various Wyndham relatives, will be staying at the Manor.' Ryder smiled at her. 'The Morton family, of course, have their own private residence.'

Anna looked down at their joined hands in silence.

'Penny for them?' said Ryder.

'I was just remembering the last time you had a marquee at the Manor. At least the last time I know about.'

'There hasn't been a marquee here since the party you ran away from.' He gave her a confident smile. 'I'll make sure you enjoy this one, Anna.'

'At least I'll have Dad and Tom for support. Last time, courtesy of a coven of teenage witches, I felt like Cinderella before the fairy godmother waved her wand.' Her eyes flashed. 'And, to top it all, you kissed me goodnight—my very first kiss by the way—then zoomed off in your new car in a tearing hurry to get back to the girls who'd ruined the party for me.'

Ryder stared at her in surprise. 'Was it really your first kiss, Anna?'

'Yes.'

'If I'd known, I would have made it more memorable.'

'It was memorable enough as it was, Ryder,' she said tartly. 'I certainly never forgot it—or anything else about that night.'

He squeezed her hand. 'This time it will be different for you, I promise. Though I'm afraid Edwina will be there again. I can't hurt her parents by leaving her off the list.'

Anna groaned. 'I had cold feet about coming before I knew that, Ryder.'

'Why? This time you'll be the belle of the ball.'

'Certainly not. That's Hannah's role. Mine is a lot lower down the cast list.'

Ryder turned her face towards him with his free hand. 'Don't tell me you're still suffering from your gamekeeper's brat complex?' he demanded, frowning.

She shrugged mutinously. 'When I'm in London I never think about it. But down here it's hard to shake off.' She tried to turn away, but Ryder held her still with a relentless finger. Blue eyes bored into resentful dark ones for a tense moment before he released her, scowling.

'Utter bloody nonsense, Anna. Hector would have come down on you like a ton of bricks if he'd known. He considered himself as good as any man and my father looked on him as a friend. I thought you and I were friends too,' he added sternly. 'We were in the old days, before you started all this rubbish about a gulf.'

Anna snatched her hand away in sudden fury, her eyes glittering into his. 'If it's rubbish, why were you so appalled at the thought of having me for a sister-in-law?'

The blue eyes lit with such sudden anger she tried to jump up to escape, but Ryder caught her hand and pulled her back down beside him. 'I've already told you that. I thought you were ditching Mansell in favour of a good-looking young stud with money to offer and the lure of a New York lifestyle as the icing on the cake. Not to mention the fact that Dominic is a Wyndham.'

'Thanks a lot! Even if any of that were true, which it was not, I'd left Sean by that time.' Anna wrenched her hand away and jumped up to glare down at him in outrage. 'You were my best friend once. How could you possibly think that?'

He looked up at her, his eyes drawn from her hostile face to the breasts heaving with temper beneath the clinging gold wool. Tendrils were escaping from the hair she'd twisted into a hasty knot after their encounter earlier, and her eyes glittered darkly in her angry, flushed face. He felt his muscles tighten in response and got to his feet, filled with a sudden heat that had nothing to do with friendship.

'That was whole point, Anna. It sounds idiotically dramatic now, but at the time I felt a sense of betrayal. Then, when I learned the truth that night—'

'You heard it earlier than that from me, but oh, no! You wouldn't believe me. It took Dominic to convince you. Can you even begin to imagine how much that hurt, Ryder?' Anna stared angrily into the intent blue eyes, her heart beating thickly with pure temper.

Suddenly she realised it was something very different from temper. As he moved closer her breath caught in her throat. This heat rushing over her came from an entirely different source and she could see it reflected in the blue eyes smouldering with answering fire. She backed away in sudden panic, but Ryder closed the gap between them and pulled her hard against him as his mouth met hers. Her lips parted involuntarily as his tongue slid between them and she gave a stifled moan as his hands moved beneath her sweater to caress bare skin. His mouth took such complete possession of hers that she was lost to everything other than the sensations setting her body alight as his skilled, seducing fingers found her breasts and teased nipples which rose erect and sensitive to his touch. When he raised his head at last they gazed at each other in tense, unbelieving silence for a moment, both of them breathing raggedly, the colour flaring along the slanting Wyndham cheekbones matching the flush on Anna's stunned face.

The silence stretched to unbearable length until at last Ryder raised a quizzical eyebrow. 'For God's sake say something, Anna.'

'That was a bit different from our first kiss,' she commented hoarsely, heart thumping. 'You've honed your skills over the years, Ryder.'

'You said you were hurt,' he said softly. 'I was just kissing you better.'

Better than anyone else in her entire life. Anna sucked in a deep, unsteady breath. 'You took me by surprise, Ryder. We've never been on kissing terms.'

'Blame it on the quarrel—and that towel,' he said ruefully.

To Anna's intense irritation she felt her colour deepen. 'I was perfectly respectable—it was a very big towel.'

'It was the insecurity rather than the size that did the damage.' He grinned suddenly, looking more like the Ryder of old. 'Old friend you might be, but you're also a very sexy lady, Anna Morton, and, as you've just found out, I'm an all too normal male. But it's not a problem. At least, not for you. You'll sleep undisturbed tonight, I promise.'

Ryder was wrong about that, Anna found later. Once they'd parted, rather awkwardly, outside her room, she got ready for bed knowing she was unlikely to fall asleep any time soon. No matter how much she tried to blank out Ryder's kiss, it was no easier to forget than the first one all those years ago. The astonishing part this time round was her response. No man in her past, Sean included, had ever set her on fire with just one kiss and a few caresses. A hungry, demanding kiss, it was true, and caresses which demonstrated very clearly that Ryder knew what he was about when it came to making love to a woman. But he'd made no attempt to go further than that, for which she was profoundly grateful because she doubted she could have resisted if he had.

She was still reeling from the shock of her instant, overwhelming arousal at the hands of a man she'd always looked on as a friend, then as an enemy, but never as a lover. She sighed impatiently. If she had any sense she'd make a run for it to Shrewsbury tomorrow. But she had to wait until the work on Keeper's Cottage was finished, she reminded herself. Another day at the Manor would do no harm and then she'd just go back to Keeper's and things would return to normal—the Squire and Anna Morton back in their respective places where they belonged.

A few doors away Ryder stared at his bedroom ceiling, also wide awake, cursing himself for giving in to the rush of desire that had suddenly overpowered him. For a few minutes there he'd wanted to throw Anna down on the sofa and take possession of her, body and soul. This was new. He'd possessed—and enjoyed—women in the past, but always with no emotions involved, no strings attached and an amicable goodbye when it came, as it always did in time, to the parting of the ways. Edwina had been the only exception and he would make damned sure he never made that particular mistake again. But after his mistake tonight Anna was probably packing right now, ready to take off in the morning.

Ryder slept at last but woke early and dressed in a hurry. As he passed Anna's door he paused, listening, but all was quiet. He went very quietly down the sweeping curve of stairs to cross the hall to the kitchen and then stopped in his tracks as he opened the door. Anna was sitting at the table drinking tea, an open book propped against the marmalade jar.

'Good morning,' he said, closing the door behind him. 'You're up early.'

She smiled at him, noting the shadows under his blue eyes, which were not nearly as brilliant as usual. He hadn't slept too well either. 'When I woke up I remembered I hadn't taken anything out of the freezer for dinner, so I got dressed and came down early to forage,' she said briskly. 'Now I'm here I'll cook breakfast for you, if you like.'

'Have you had yours?'

'No. Just tea.'

'Then let's both have breakfast. You cook, I'll make the toast and pour the orange juice,' he said, relieved. Anna obviously had no immediate plans to leave.

'I suppose that's your idea of fair division of labour, Squire,' she said, shaking her head, and tucked a bookmark into her novel. 'All right. But only because it's so early.'

'What difference does that make?' he demanded, handing her a frying pan.

'So I can clear away and have everything shipshape by the time Carol and her gang get here.' Anna pulled a face. 'I'd hate Mrs Carter to hear I hadn't been looking after you properly.'

'You're not supposed to be looking after me,' he pointed out. 'You're the one who's been ill. I should be looking after you.'

'Stop arguing and fetch me the eggs,' she ordered as she searched in the fridge for bacon. 'I noticed a new supply in the scullery. Do you keep chickens now?'

'No. I buy them from Dick Hammond. At the recommended retail price,' Ryder added pointedly.

'Good for you.'

Anna soon put plates of bacon and eggs on the table, so pleased to be back on a normal footing after the episode of the night before that she fell on the food with almost as much gusto as Ryder.

'This is an unexpected treat. I came down early to take a cup of tea up to you,' he informed her as they ate. 'But you'd beaten me to it.'

'What time does Mrs Carter get here in the morning?'

'Eight-thirty. I'm usually out and about by then.' Ryder gave her a stern look as he laid down his knife and fork. 'Take it easy today. Don't bother about the arrangements for the ball.'

She gave him a non-committal smile, secretly resolved to have everything sorted by the time Ryder got home. 'Can you give me Mrs Carter's number? I'll have a chat with her later on.'

'It's keyed in on the phone. And you already have mine, so ring me if you need me.'

'With all the help here at hand, I doubt that I will,' she assured him and got up to clear away. 'Right. I hate to rush you, Squire, but I must have this place sparkling before Carol and her gang arrive.'

Ryder swallowed the last of his coffee and got up. 'That was just what I needed, Anna. My compliments to the chef. I had a look at the pups yesterday, by the way. They're growing fast.'

'Give them a kiss for me next time you see them,' she said promptly.

He laughed. 'And have Jen thinking I was losing my marbles? Bob Godfrey won't be here today, by the way; he's going to a funeral, so I told the lads to take a day off. Have a good day, Miss Morton.'

'You too, Squire. What time will you be home?'

'I'm still doing my bit with the new fencing, so I'm not sure. I'll ring you when I'm on my way.' He smiled as he made for the door. 'See you later, Anna.'

She stood still for a moment, gazing at the door he closed behind him, then took a deep breath, pushed all thought of Ryder Wyndham from her mind and set to work.

When the cleaners arrived the kitchen was as spotless as an operating theatre, and after the greetings were over Anna went straight to the office. She called up the file Ryder had made for the ball arrangements and got to work. By the time Alison brought her a cup of coffee, Anna had spoken to all the suppliers, requested emails in confirmation, printed them off to show Ryder and felt satisfied that everything was going to plan for what was obviously an event of some importance in the locality.

'I'm just about to ring Mrs Carter,' she told Alison and smiled. 'Any message?'

'Tell her we're all working our fingers to the bone,' said Alison promptly, 'and we hope she's feeling better.'

Mrs Carter was feeling a lot better, she told Anna. 'I'm coming back tomorrow, dear, so tell those girls I'll be checking up on them.'

'They're doing a splendid job,' Anna assured her. 'Are you really well enough to come back so soon? Ryder was very concerned about you yesterday.'

'Only because of the sneezing. I'm not infectious now. How are you, Anna?'

'I'm fine. See you tomorrow, then.'

After she rang off, Anna contacted Brian, who told her the cottage would be ready by the afternoon.

'You can move back in any time you like after that, Miss Morton. I'll call round to the Manor with the keys later and explain how the alarm system works.'

She thanked him warmly, asked him to bring his bill with him and then went back to transferring Ryder's files, an occupation which absorbed her so completely that she looked up in surprise when Carol appeared to say it was one o'clock and time she took a break for lunch.

'We're off now,' she said. 'Would you like to check on what we've done?'

'No, indeed, I'm sure everything's perfect.'

'We changed the sheets on the bed in the blue room and cleaned the bathroom, but we didn't move your things.'

'I should have told you I'm only here for one more night,' said Anna with remorse. 'You could have left the bed. Sorry, Carol.'

'Not a problem,' said the woman cheerfully. 'A sheet or two extra won't hurt us. Brian's finished the work on Keeper's Cottage, then?'

'Yes. I can move back tomorrow.'

Anna smiled wryly as she made herself a sandwich later. The village grapevine was in perfect working order as usual. Everyone knew about the burglary and now they would know that Keeper's Cottage was secure, which was good. They also knew that Anna was occupying one of the guest rooms at the

Manor, not sharing with Ryder. She shrugged. On the other hand, probably no one thought for a moment that this was likely where the Squire and Anna Morton were concerned.

After Brian called with the keys and gave her a swift course of instruction on the alarm system, Anna spent the rest of the afternoon working in the office. But this time she finished early enough to make sure she was showered and fully dressed long before Ryder was due home. Wrapped in one of Mrs Carter's voluminous white aprons to protect her scarlet sweater and the black jeans she was very tired of by this time, she peeled potatoes and put them in to roast. She kept herself busy, but she was very glad when Ryder rang at five-thirty to tell her he was on his way. The Manor was not a house she was comfortable alone in for any length of time, which was why she'd kept to the office as long as possible.

Ryder grinned as he came into the kitchen a few minutes later. 'Damn. You've got your clothes on today!'

She laughed. 'Pre-warned is pre-armed. Have you been labouring again?'

'Long and hard,' he assured her. 'I'll open more of the Barolo we drank last night to go with dinner. Give me half an hour and I'll be with you.'

'I hope you don't mind having so many lights on upstairs.' She smiled crookedly. 'I tend to get a bit nervous here on my own once the daylight goes.'

Ryder gave her a straight look. 'You can do exactly as you like here, Anna. My house is your house, as the saying goes. And, just so you know, there are no ghosts here that I've ever heard about.'

CHAPTER EIGHT

DINNER was over and they were sitting in front of the fire in the morning room before Anna told Ryder she was going back to Keeper's the next day. 'Mrs Carter insists on coming back tomorrow and the cottage is ready, so there's no need for me to stay longer. Brian brought the keys round this afternoon.'

'You waited until I was softened up with good food and wine before you told me that,' he accused.

'Why should I need to soften you up?'

'You knew I wouldn't be pleased by the news.'

She shook her head. 'It never occurred to me. It was very kind of you to let me stay here, but I'm sure you'd like the house to yourself again.'

He touched her hand fleetingly. 'You're wrong, Anna. I'll miss you.'

'You're too busy for that,' she said lightly and changed the subject to tell him that all was proceeding smoothly with the arrangements for the ball. 'I received emails in confirmation from all the firms concerned, so you can refer to them if you need to check. After that I did a bit more work on your files.'

'What an independent creature you are,' he said, shaking his head.

'Why do you say that?'

'You just had to do something in return for board and lodging, didn't you, Anna?'

'I was glad to have something to do.'

'It never occurred to you to curl up with a book in here, or watch daytime television?'

'I'll probably do that back at the cottage, but I wouldn't have been comfortable doing it here. Your reputation's safe, by the way,' she added. 'Carol and the gang know I occupied a guest room.'

He gave her an evil smile. 'And what, exactly, was going to prevent me from walking a few yards from my room to yours, should the fancy take me?'

'No one would think for a moment that the Squire would have designs on someone like me!'

'*You* know damn well that I do,' he said roughly and, before she knew what he had in mind, Ryder scooped her up on to his lap and pulled her hard against him as he kissed her. Anna made a stifled sound of protest, but he merely deepened the kiss and held her captive when she tried to move. This was her old friend Ryder, her brain told her, but her body knew from the erection she could feel stirring against her thighs that he now wanted to be her lover. His mouth and tongue and caressing hands conjured up magic which blew her mind so completely she responded with total abandon for a hot throbbing interval that left them breathless and shaken when Anna tore her mouth away at last.

'Ryder,' she said hoarsely, as she stared up into the blue eyes blazing with such heat that she swallowed hard, 'we're just friends. This isn't supposed to happen to us.'

He kissed her again. 'Why not? I'm a man and,' he added, a note in his voice which sent a shiver up her spine as he trailed a hand across her breasts, 'you are most definitely a woman. I want you, Anna.'

'You mean you want to sleep with me?'

His eyes gleamed. 'Only after I've made love to you for a very long time.'

'I can't take this in.' She shook her head, trying to make her brain work. 'This is all a bit sudden, Ryder.'

'Sudden? We've known each other for twenty-five years,' he said, laughing.

'But just as friends.'

'True. I thought of you that way too. Right up to the time Dominic came home from London so smitten with your charms I wanted to hit him. Why do you think I gave you such hell when I thought you were going to marry him?'

'You've already explained that,' she said, suddenly in command of herself again. She tried to sit up, but Ryder held her fast.

'There was more to it than that, Anna.'

In no mood for a wrestling match she knew she would lose, she looked up into the blue eyes gleaming with a disturbingly possessive look. 'So tell me, then.'

'I was jealous.' He shrugged. 'Laugh if you like. I'd never experienced that particular emotion, so I needed to hit out at someone.'

'And the lucky someone was me,' said Anna bitterly. 'I couldn't believe it when you snarled at me like that.'

'For me it was a case of snarling or kissing you senseless, darling.'

Darling? She bit her lip, shaken, and Ryder kissed her again, sliding his tongue over her bottom lip. He cradled her against him, the kiss progressing from gentle to incendiary so quickly they were soon on fire, her hands as importunate as his as they kissed and caressed each other into a state of desperation.

'You see?' he said hoarsely at last. 'Admit it, Anna. You want me as much as I want you.'

She buried her face against his chest. 'I do. But I just can't believe that you're the man making me feel like this. It's never happened to me before.'

He took in a deep breath and turned her face up to his. 'Is that true?'

'I don't lie, Ryder,' she said impatiently.

He kissed her in passionate appreciation, then raised his head to give her a smile which made her heart flip over in her chest. 'Come to bed with me, Anna.'

Careful, she told herself. 'Ryder, we've been friends for so long I need time to get used to you as a lover.' She gave him a wry little smile. 'I've never had one before.'

He frowned. 'Then how did you classify Mansell?'

'Boyfriend, like the others. Sean's only difference was his persistence. He wore me down until I gave in and moved in with him.' She touched a hand to his cheek. 'You, on the other hand, are all too easy to think of as a lover now the subject's come up.'

Ryder eyed her with interest. 'So what, exactly, are my qualifications for the post?'

Anna pretended to think it over. 'I suppose it has a lot to do with that traffic-stopping face of yours, and the great body.'

'Stop teasing, Anna Morton. It was a serious question.'

'It was a serious answer.' She touched a hand to his cheek. 'You're a supremely attractive man, Ryder, in every way. Surely the conveyor belt crowd must have convinced you of that?'

He shrugged dismissively. 'The looks probably helped, but the real attraction for all of them, Edwina included, was my life-style—or, to reduce it to basic terms, the money that went with it.'

Anna promptly described Edwina in a few basic terms which brought a crack of delighted laugher from Ryder. 'Tut, tut, Miss Morton. If your grandfather could hear you now.'

'Actually Gramp agreed with me. In his opinion, that young woman of yours—I quote—didn't deserve such excellent husband material.' She fluttered her eyelashes.

Ryder grimaced. 'If he'd suspected I wanted to be *your* lover, though, he would have come after me with a shotgun.'

Anna shook her head, chuckling. 'He handed that over to Dad a long time ago.'

'I'd better be careful around Dr Morton too, then—both doctors Morton.' He traced a finger over her bottom lip and clenched his teeth as she bit gently on his fingertip. 'I'd rather they didn't know about my sudden desperation to take you to bed.' He kissed the palm of her hand and closed her fingers over it. 'That's between you and me alone, Anna.'

'Very definitely.' She looked up at him in wonder. 'Ryder, I can't believe that we're actually sitting her discussing the possibility of becoming lovers.'

'Certainty, not possibility. But since that's obviously not going to happen tonight,' he said with deep regret, 'I shall now escort you upstairs to your bed and try to get to sleep in my own.'

Anna waited while Ryder checked that all was secure and then went upstairs with him to the blue room. He paused outside the door, then took her in his arms and kissed her goodnight. She stood on tiptoe to return the kiss with a warmth that sent the blood rushing from his brain to other parts of him less easy to control as he crushed her close for a moment or two before he let her go. She stood back, staring at him, dazed.

'This is so weird, Ryder. Yesterday we were just good friends, today we could be two different people.'

'Just think what can happen tomorrow!'

'I'm leaving tomorrow,' she reminded him.

'Don't think you can escape that easily. I'll come over to see you after dinner. To make sure the work's been done properly on the cottage,' he added virtuously and grinned, a light in his eyes that made her toes curl. 'And to check on a few other things.'

'Such as?'

'I'll tell you when I see you. Goodnight, my darling. Sleep well.'

After packing her few belongings, Anna slept far better than expected and got up early to strip the bed and tidy the room. When Ryder came along the landing, yawning, he picked up her suitcase, eyeing her morosely.

'Can't wait to make your getaway, I suppose.'

'I wanted to be ready before Mrs Carter turns up. Good morning, Ryder,' she added sweetly. 'Did you sleep well?'

He gave her a jaundiced look. 'No. Did you?'

'I did, actually.'

'Lucky you.'

Anna smiled demurely. 'Want some breakfast?' she asked as they reached the kitchen.

He brightened. 'Now you're talking.'

Because Ryder wanted to see Mrs Carter before taking off for the day, they lingered over the meal, taking such pleasure over it that Anna admitted she could get to like breakfast in these circumstances.

'I don't bother much in London. I get something on the way to the office,' she confessed.

'I did the same in my City days,' he agreed and smiled at her. 'This kind of meal never happened during that period of my life. The women I knew weren't the kind I wanted to face across a breakfast table next morning.'

'Your playmates weren't the domesticated kind?'

He shook his head. 'If any of them knew how to cook they never admitted it.'

Anna glanced up at the kitchen clock. 'Time for one more cup of coffee, then I must get busy. I want this place immaculate before Mrs Carter arrives.'

'I'll help,' Ryder offered, but she shook her head.

'If she found you washing up she'd never speak to me again.'

'I do it at the weekend. At least, I stuff everything in the dishwasher,' he amended honestly.

'Not today. I'll do it. Check your emails if you want something to do.'

'I'd rather hang around here and watch you, Anna. Kiss me goodbye now, while we're still alone.'

When Mrs Carter arrived, laden with bags, she was full of apologies for her absence and said she was perfectly well when asked about her cold. When she'd taken her coat off she offered to cook breakfast for Ryder before he went out.

'No need, Martha. Anna's already done that.'

'Splendid,' said Mrs Carter in approval, eyeing her. 'I hope you ate some as well, dear. You're still very thin.'

Anna assured her she had, then said it was time she went home.

'I hope you're not leaving just because I'm back, Anna?'

'No. I want to clean the cottage properly now the repairs have been done. My father's coming at the weekend.'

'Don't work too hard, dear, and mind you eat.' She put a loaf of bread in a bag. 'I baked yesterday, so take this with you, Anna.'

'Thank you, Mrs Carter, I adore your bread. Give my regards to Carol and the others.'

'I'll carry your bag for you, Anna,' said Ryder. He went outside with her, stowed the bag in the boot of her car, then straightened, his back to the kitchen windows. 'I'll see you tonight—after my solitary meal.' The look in his eyes set her pulse racing. 'I'll miss my dinner companion.'

'We'll have coffee together instead,' she offered.

'I'll look forward to it. And Martha's right. Don't do too much today.'

She rolled her eyes as she got in the car. 'I'm fine now, Ryder. See you later.'

It took more of an effort than Anna expected to unlock the door of Keeper's Cottage. As she keyed in the code on her new alarm she made a conscious decision that no intruder must be allowed to spoil her pleasure in her home. But as she went on a tour of inspection to see what needed to be done, her eyes widened in surprise. The whole house was immaculate. And, other than the smell of fresh paint and the new lock on the window in the spare room, there was no trace of the break-in. If the pictures and plates hadn't been missing from the sitting room, Anna would have thought she'd imagined the whole thing.

She rang the number Brian had given her and thanked him for doing such a good job. 'But who did the cleaning?'

'Squire asked me to find someone reliable to do it for you, so my wife volunteered. Emma had to wash the curtains from the spare room, by the way. I hope that's all right.'

'It's a lot more than all right, Brian, it all looks wonderful. Please convey my grateful thanks to Emma.' She hesitated, hoping she wasn't going to cause offence. 'How much do I owe her?'

'Squire saw to all that, Miss Morton.'

After more fervent thanks, Anna rang off. She would take it up with 'Squire' later. Ryder Wyndham was a sight too high-handed at times, downright interfering, in fact. But, on the plus side, she could now get straight on with some laundry and then go down to the village to buy food.

To her surprise, Anna found she was sorry there'd been no cleaning to do. Once she'd hung out her washing and driven down to the village to shop, she had nothing to do until she could get on with the ironing. Tonight she'd ask Ryder if she could carry on with his files until she left. She could keep on top of arrangements for the ball at the same time.

For lunch she scrambled eggs to eat with toast made from Mrs Carter's matchless bread, then did her ironing and at last settled down with a book for a rest, something she'd been neglecting during her stay at the Manor. But as time passed by with relentless lack of speed Anna felt excitement mounting inside her at the thought of seeing Ryder again. Which was utterly astonishing. A few kisses were all it had taken to wake her up to the fact that her feelings for him were not only anything but platonic any more, they were also quite different from anything she'd felt for a man in the past.

She'd had a fair number of boyfriends in her time. Not that the body count had been high. Casual, light-hearted romances in college had been succeeded by more of the same when she found her first job. But none of them had made much of a mark until she met Sean Mansell, who had stood out from the rest due to his remorseless, flattering pursuit. But she should have known, thought Anna morosely, that her relationship with Sean had no hope of surviving the reality of living together.

And all along Ryder Wyndham had been there in the background of her life, his looks and personality and everything else he had going for him the benchmark by which she'd subconsciously judged all other men. Why had it taken until now to admit it? Not that it would have done her any good if she had. After the turning point of his eighteenth birthday party, she'd decided it was best to avoid him as much as possible. She knew Ryder had been hurt by her withdrawal and in secret she'd shed a lot of tears because she missed him so much. The men in her family had been utterly mystified by her U-turn and when she refused to discuss it put it down to teenage hormones. But Anna had always listened avidly when Hector passed on all the latest news about Ryder. Tom had also kept in constant touch with Ryder over the years and took great pleasure in telling Anna about the constant stream of female talent in Ryder's life. She'd listened with outward indifference, secretly hungry for all the news she could get. But she'd been utterly appalled when Tom broke the news about Edwina French. Anna had tried to convince herself that her reaction was natural disappointment over Ryder's choice of bride, but in reality it had been basic jealousy—red in tooth and claw. It had been her belief that Ryder was still engaged to Edwina that made her so adamant about rejecting his apologies. But now, thank God, Edwina was no longer part of his life. Anna smiled happily at the thought and went upstairs to spend an outrageously long time getting ready for Ryder's visit later.

She took so long over the process that she had only just finished the sandwich she'd made for her supper when the phone rang.

'Anna,' said Ryder, 'I'm on my way.'

'You're early!'

'And impatient,' he said in a tone which sent her totally haywire.

Anna forced herself to sit in the parlour to listen for the car. She stared at a newscast on television without taking in a word of it and tried to read instead. She gave it up after a page or two, wondering why Ryder was taking so long to drive such a short distance. At last she heard the doorbell and ran to throw open the door. Ryder backed her inside, thrust the door shut and pulled her into his arms, his mouth devouring hers in a kiss that buckled her knees.

'Hi,' she said faintly, when he raised his head.

He smiled, the gleam in his eyes doing serious damage to her heart rate. 'Good evening, Miss Morton, I trust I find you well?'

'Yes. I didn't hear the car.'

He smiled again, in triumph this time. 'I walked.'

'Why?'

'I thought you might not want my car at your gate for hours. This way I can stay.'

'Until when, exactly?'

'Until you say it's time for me to go.' He stroked her cheek. 'But be warned, Anna. I'm not always this tame.'

'I'll keep that in mind.'

'Not,' he said gruffly, 'that I feel very tame right now.' His eyes smouldered into hers for an instant before his mouth came down on hers as he caught her close.

Her lips parted in response and the kiss deepened and grew fierce as his hands pushed wool and satin aside to find her breasts. Her back arched as he moved his lips down her throat and she gave a stifled moan as his fingers teased nipples which rose erect and sensitised, sending darts of fire along every nerve. When he raised his head they gazed at each other in taut silence for a moment.

'I want you, Anna. For God's sake say you want me.'

'Of course I want you,' she said impatiently. 'Let's go to bed.'

Ryder gave a choked laugh, then seized her hand, half dragging her as they made for the stairs, both of them stumbling a little in the narrow space in their hurry to get to the top. When they finally made it, Ryder pushed her against the wall and held her there for a long moment, his mouth hot on hers, and Anna locked her arms round him, returning the kiss with abandon. She felt him harden against her through their clothes and with a gasp broke free to pull him into her room. She'd left a lamp burning by the bed. Ryder sat down on the edge of the bed and drew her down on his lap, stifling a groan when she wriggled against him.

'If you do that, you risk consequences,' he warned huskily, his hands caressing her back.

'I'm counting on it.' She heaved in a deep unsteady breath. 'So get your clothes off.'

Ryder stood her on her feet and kissed her long and hard. 'I'll get your clothes off first.'

He stripped off her sweater, but, instead of caressing her, he stood very still, looking down at her with possessive eyes that hardened her nipples as though he'd touched her. She felt her face burn, along with other parts that ought to have felt cold as he removed everything else she had on, his hands unsteady in their haste.

'Now you,' she said breathlessly. 'Or do you need help?'

Ryder shook his head and got rid of his clothes at such speed that Anna had no time to admire the muscular body before it was pressed close to hers, holding her still as he kissed her.

'You must know,' he said against her mouth, his voice deep and hoarse with need, 'that I want you so much I can hardly breathe.'

'I can't either,' she gasped.

He groaned like a man in pain and laid her on the bed. 'If it kills me, I'm going to take my time over this. I want to savour every moment.' He smiled into her eyes as he let himself down beside her. 'But I have a slight problem with that. Now we're naked together I may possibly explode if I don't have you within the next few seconds.'

'Then stop talking!'

Ryder let out a deep, delighted laugh and kissed her and she reached up her hands to thrust them through the black curls that were already damp from the effort he was making to take things slowly. But Anna wanted him to lose control. She wanted passion and heat and dug her fingers into his shoulders, her breath quickening as she felt his erection nudge the part of her that was ready and waiting for him. They kissed wildly until they could no longer breathe, then he slid his lips down her throat in swift, drinking motion; his hair brushing her skin as he moved lower to caress her nipples with lips and fingers; then lower still to test her readiness with caresses which won him a frenzied response. Ryder leaned away from her to reach down into a pocket, but she pulled him back, shaking her head, and he smiled into her eyes as he hung over her for a moment, then sheathed himself to the hilt in her tight, wet warmth.

The glorious jolt of sensation held them stunned and still for a brief, breathless moment before Ryder began to move. Anna moved with him, her body adjusting to the rhythm as though it had been created for the sole purpose of mating with the man giving her such heart-stopping pleasure. She revelled in the mounting heat and thrust and glorious earthiness of it as he buried his face in her hair, whispering gratifying, incendiary words in her ear until at last he slid his hands beneath her hips, raising her to take the full force of all he had to give, and she cooperated with total abandon, revolving her hips against him to experience every last nuance of sensation. She gave a stifled cry and dug her nails into his back, clenching her inner muscles around him in fierce possession as they reached the ultimate peak of physical rapture.

Ryder Wyndham had made love to enough women to know which of them achieved orgasm in his arms and those who gave Oscar-winning performances while pretending they did. With Anna the entire experience was so different from any other that he marvelled that his childhood friend should be the first woman in his life to fulfil his dreams of the passionate, generous lover all men fantasised about.

'I don't need to ask how it was for you,' he said when he raised his head at last.

'Why?' she said drowsily. 'I didn't say anything.'

'You didn't tell me with your voice.'

'Are you being crude, Ryder Wyndham?'

'No. How could anything as perfect as that be crude?' He preened shamelessly. 'I gave my woman pleasure and I'm proud of it.'

She frowned. 'Is that what I am?'

'My woman? Of course you are. Any argument?'

Anna gazed at him with heavy eyes that looked even darker than usual due to pupils dilated by her recent activity. 'My brain has taken time out so I can't think of one right now.'

Ryder heaved over on his back, taking her with him to lie in the crook of his arm.

She turned her face up to look at him. 'That was unreal, Ryder.'

'Not unreal. Sublime.' He breathed in deeply. 'Unlike Violet and Ned we're alive, so let's take full advantage of the fact.'

Anna levered herself up on an elbow to look down into his face. 'What do you mean?'

Ryder's eyes held hers. 'You belong to me, Anna. Admit it.'

She swallowed. 'Does the reverse apply?'

'Of course I belong to you. I have in some ways since I was eleven years old.'

'How about Edwina and the rest?'

'How about Mansell and the rest?' he countered and pulled her down to lie on top of him. 'They were just past diversions on a road which led back to each other. There'll be no more diversions,' he added sternly. 'From now on it's only you, Anna.'

She looked down into the familiar handsome face and felt a rush of feeling so intense she was afraid to trust her voice for a moment.

'Say it,' he ordered, his voice cracking slightly.

'Only you, Ryder.'

He turned over, rolling her beneath him. 'Now convince me you mean that—without words.'

It was midnight before Ryder heaved himself out of bed. 'I hate the very thought of it, but I really must go.' He thrust a hand through his wildly tousled hair and began pulling on his clothes.

Anna slid to her feet and wrapped herself in her dressing gown. 'Worse still, you have to walk home too. Have some coffee first.'

He gave her a heavy-lidded look which brought heat rushing to her face. 'My darling, if I do I'll want to come back to bed.'

Shaken by how much she wanted that too, Anna went downstairs with him. 'Ring me when you get home,' she ordered as Ryder kissed her goodnight at the front door.

'You could be asleep by that time, Anna.'

She shook her head. 'Not until I know you're home safely.'

'So you do care for me,' he said with satisfaction.

She gave him a slow smile. 'I thought I'd proved that pretty conclusively this evening, Ryder Wyndham!'

His eyes glinted. 'Prove it to me again tomorrow.'

'Are we seeing each other tomorrow?'

'Of course we are.'

She smiled. 'In that case, give Mrs Carter a night off and come to supper.'

For answer Ryder kissed her hard. 'I must *go,*' he groaned. 'Lock up behind me. Goodnight, darling, sleep well.'

Not much doubt about that, thought Anna, as she went back upstairs. She might have spent the entire evening in bed but there'd been no sleep involved. Making love with Ryder Wyndham had been exhilarating, wildly passionate and yet at the same time light-hearted and such *fun*—totally unlike anything Anna had encountered before. While she tidied the bed she felt embarrassed now to think she'd once imagined herself in love with Sean Mansell. It had been a fizzy lemonade affair compared to the vintage champagne of her feelings for Ryder. She had a strong suspicion she was falling in love with a man she'd known since she was eight years old. It half thrilled her, half scared her to death. She grabbed her phone when it rang, her eyes shining as she heard Ryder's voice.

'Just reporting in, Anna,' he said caressingly. 'So you can go to sleep now.'

'I've got something to do first.'

'Why didn't you say? I could have done it for you before I left.'

Anna chuckled. 'There's not much you can do about the bath I'm about to wallow in.'

'Except wallow in it with you.' He groaned. 'I really wish you hadn't told me that. I'll lie awake for hours, picturing it.'

'Try counting sheep.'

'I'd rather think of you.'

'Likewise, Ryder,' she assured him. 'But I have a bone to pick with you, Squire. In the heat of the moment tonight—well, several moments, really—I forgot that I was annoyed with you.'

'Why? What have I done?'

'You paid Brian's wife to clean my cottage. If you'll tell me how much she charged I'll pay you.'

'Certainly,' he said promptly, surprising her. 'She was very expensive. You owe me big time. But I want kisses for payment, not money.'

'Are you sure you mean kisses?' she said, chuckling.

'I'll take anything you have to offer!'

Anna slept well and woke late next morning, glad because it shortened the time until she saw Ryder again. She shook her head in amazement. She was behaving like a teenager with a first romance. She lingered over a late breakfast and then drove to the village to buy food for dinner. When she got home she spent a shameless amount of time on her appearance and shamelessly little on preparing dinner. She'd decided to serve Ryder a cold meal, for reasons she was embarrassed to admit to herself, but which proved to be only practical when he made it patently obvious he wanted to take her to bed as soon as he arrived.

'We can eat later if you like,' she offered, when he let her go after a protracted kiss of greeting.

'Of course I like. Dinner won't spoil?' he demanded.

She shook her head. 'It can wait.'

'Excellent, because I can't,' he said, taking her hand to make for the stairs.

This time Ryder was so hungry for her that Anna lay dazed and gasping afterwards.

'I'd been thinking about that all day, so I was in a hurry. I promise to do better next time,' he said, stroking a gentling hand down her spine.

'I don't think I can cope with better,' she said faintly and Ryder smoothed her tumbled hair, his eyes glittering with remorse.

'Did I hurt you?'

'Not in the least.' She gave him a glinting, satisfied smile. 'It was quite wonderful to be wanted so badly.'

'Only by me,' he commanded.

'Only you, Ryder,' she assured him and pushed at his encircling arms. 'Now let me up. We need to refuel. Fancy a picnic in the parlour?'

Ryder went downstairs with her to help, barefoot in jeans and sweater, Anna in her dressing gown and the famous sheepskin slippers. She explained their provenance as she loaded a tray with the dishes she had ready in the refrigerator.

'Hector was a man of great common sense,' he agreed, lips twitching. 'I noticed the slippers the first evening I called here.'

'I could tell, which is why I didn't ask my favour there and then. I was determined to look more appealing while I did my wheedling.'

'You appeal to me whatever you wear, especially an insecure towel.' He gave her a smile which brought heat rushing to her cheeks. 'But you appeal to me most with no clothes at all.'

'Typical man,' she said darkly and checked on the tray. 'Smoked salmon, Parma ham, potato salad, green salad, French dressing. Right, you take the tray, Ryder, I'll bring the rest.'

They sat close together to eat, both of them so hungry that the food disappeared in record time.

Ryder refilled their wineglasses, put an arm round her waist and sat back with a sigh of pleasure. 'I came early for two reasons. First and most important, I couldn't wait to make sure last night wasn't a figment of my fevered imagination, and second, I have to be up at dawn tomorrow. New drainage pipes are going in at the bottom of Long Acre.'

Anna wriggled closer and he turned to look at her. 'I could soon get used to this, Anna.'

She made no pretence of misunderstanding. 'Having someone to talk to?'

'Exactly. I spend a lot of evenings poring over accounts or catching up with my emails. This evening, for reasons which are obvious, is a huge improvement.'

'If that's a compliment, thank you. But, talking of emails, are the plans for the ball coming along well?'

He nodded. 'Due to your efficiency, they most certainly are.'

'Just one thing, though, Ryder. It struck me this morning that there was no mention of flowers.'

'It's a ball, not a wedding, Anna!'

'You've ordered a marquee with top of the range chandeliers and stars on a midnight-blue ceiling, so in my humble opinion you need flowers—'

'*Humble!*' said Ryder, laughing. 'You don't do humble either, Anna. So where do you want to put these flowers?'

'On the tables in the marquee as centrepieces. And drinks will be served in the hall when people arrive, so a spectacular arrangement in the urn at the foot of the stairs would look good. Some guests are bound to overflow into the drawing room, so a few arrangements should go in there too.'

'I should have thought of it myself earlier,' he said, frowning.

'Why not get the flowers done locally?' suggested Anna.

'It would certainly be good PR,' he said slowly, thinking about it. 'Who do you have in mind?'

'Mrs Jessop and her team of flower arrangers. I saw their handiwork when I was in the church. I promise you'll be impressed, Ryder.'

'I am already, and not just by the flowers.' He kissed her by way of appreciation 'You're a marvel.'

'Of course I am. I'll see Mrs Jessop tomorrow and see how she feels about it.'

'You're supposed to be convalescing,' he said sternly.

'Not something you remembered earlier on,' she pointed out.

He gave her a lascivious grin. 'You didn't remind me, either.'

Mrs Jessop was delighted with the idea. 'My helpers will be thrilled to do flowers for the Squire. Ryder's very popular, Anna—far more approachable than his brother, God rest his soul.'

'Money's no object, Mrs Jessop, but I could ask Ryder about preferences and colours and so on, if you like.'

'That would help. By the way, have you met Dominic's fiancée, Anna?'

'No, but I gather she's a darling.'

'Oliver and I were very taken with her when she came to look round the church with Dominic.' Helen Jessop sighed. 'It was heart-warming to meet a couple so much in love.' She gave Anna a rather diffident look. 'Which reminds me, did you tell Ryder about your discovery in the church?'

'I certainly did.' Anna smiled ruefully. 'It was quite a shock to find his great-uncle might have been Violet's lover. Though there's no real proof, of course.'

'There might be, somewhere. Ned wrote that he was grateful for Violet's letters, so they might still be in existence. Captain Wyndham's effects would have been sent home to his family, I'm sure.'

'Of course—you're right,' said Anna, her eyes lighting up. 'I'll ask Ryder.'

Helen Jessop looked uncomfortable. 'In that case, please say it's your idea. I would hate him to think I'm intruding on his private family affairs. I've always liked Ryder enormously, Anna, and Oliver and I both have great respect for the way he's shouldered his responsibilities.' Her eyes twinkled suddenly.

'Mind you, he was quite a lad at one time. What do they call it these days—a babe magnet? A man with his looks could hardly fail to be. He's settled down a bit now, but there's no one more irresistible than a reformed rake.'

CHAPTER NINE

ANNA rang Ryder to say her mission was successful, then drove straight from the vicarage to the Manor to wait for him as he wanted. 'Ryder's still down at Long Acre, Mrs Carter, so he asked me to come here to wait for him.'

'In that case, dear, I'll get off. Young Farmers are putting on a show in the village hall tonight and I want to get there early for a good seat.'

'Sounds like fun. Have a good time.'

Mrs Carter smiled warmly. 'It's lovely to see you running in and out of here again, Anna, and it's so good for Mr Ryder. You two spent such a lot of time together in the school holidays.'

'My brother was usually around too!'

'And a nice lad he was. I can't believe he's all grown up and a surgeon now.' Mrs Carter took a look at the clock and hurried to put on her coat. 'I'll leave you to put supper on for him, then. He asked for a light meal he could see to himself so I made a spinach and bacon tart. You'll find plenty of salad ingredients in the fridge and cake in the tin as usual.'

'Don't worry. I'll look after Ryder for you,' Anna promised, smiling. 'Enjoy yourself.'

Alone again in the house, Anna overcame her qualms and went into the hall to think about flower arrangements. The vast ceramic urn would be the focal point at the foot of the stairs, which curved up above a marble floor which reflected the great

chandelier overhead. Pairs of wide mahogany doors led off the
hall at intervals, one pair into a dining room which Martha and
her helpers kept immaculate, as though the twelve William IV
chairs and long mahogany table were in use every day. A big
flower arrangement would look good on the table and side-
boards in there, she decided, and smaller ones on the numerous
gilt tables in the drawing room, which looked ghostly in the
fading light, with great mirrors over the twin fireplaces reflect-
ing the carved gilt backs of brocade sofas and chairs. Anna
backed out hurriedly, glad to return to the more homely territory of the kitchen. When she heard the Land Rover a moment
later she ran to open the door to greet Ryder, her heart doing a
forward roll in her chest when his handsome face lit up at the
sight of her.

'This is good,' he said, pulling her into his arms.

'What?'

'Coming home to you.' He took his time over kissing her, but
at last Anna pushed him away. 'What's wrong?' he demanded.

'Nothing, I just need to make my report. I'm flushed with my
success,' she told him and gave him the results of her meeting
with Helen Jessop.

Ryder smiled, impressed. 'So there's nothing left for me to do?'

'Not so fast—you don't get off scot-free,' she said, laughing.
'You have to choose which flowers and colour theme you want.'

'Hell, I thought it was too good to last.' He eyed her hopefully. 'I don't suppose you'd sort it for me?'

'Of course I could, if you're confident about my taste.'

'I trust it implicitly, Anna.'

'I'll run through a few ideas with you this evening then, and
pass them on. By the way,' added Anna, in sudden excitement,
'Mrs Jessop gave me an idea.' She stopped, biting her lip. 'If you
don't like it, please say so. It's your call.'

He sat down at the table and pulled her on his knee. 'Explain.'

'It's a bit of a long shot, but it's just possible that we might
be able to prove that Violet's lover really was your great-uncle.

Ned mentioned her letters, so maybe they came back with his belongings.' Anna kissed him fleetingly. 'Would they still be here somewhere?'

'God knows. Do that again.'

Anna obliged, letting her mouth linger and the tip of her tongue trace his lips, exulting when he crushed her close to return the compliment. Ryder raised his head at last, his eyes hot on hers. 'If I take you to explore the attics I want a reward.'

'What would you like?'

'I would like,' he said very deliberately, his breath warm against her cheek, 'to carry you off to my bed afterwards.'

'I'd like that too,' she whispered. 'I'd like it a lot.'

Ryder set her on her feet and jumped up, holding out his hand. 'Then let's do that now and explore later.'

She shook her head sternly. 'Not a chance. First the penny, then the bun, Ryder Wyndham.'

'I just love it when you're strict,' he said with relish. 'Come with me, then.'

'I hope the lights are working up there.'

'I'll go first to make sure.'

Tense with anticipation, Anna followed Ryder up the narrow stairs which led past his old room to the top attic floor where servants had lived in the Regency heyday of the house. Ryder led Anna past a series of small rooms which housed old bed-steads and pieces of furniture to a box room packed with trunks and heavy leather luggage.

'If Ned's effects were sent back, this is the most likely place. That was mine,' he said, indicating a school trunk with R.F. WYNDHAM stencilled on its lid.

'What's the F for?' asked Anna.

'Francis.'

'Like Ned,' she said, shivering a little.

Ryder put his arm round her and kissed her. 'It's cold up here. You should go down.'

But Anna's attention was on the suitcases stacked against

the walls. 'They all have initials on them. Look for one marked E.F.R.W.' She gave him a challenging smile. 'No pain, no gain, Ryder.'

He gave a long-suffering sigh. 'Oh, all right. I'll take the top layer down so you can look at the stuff below.'

The search had an unexpected result. The dust that was never allowed in the rest of the house was by no means thick in the attic room, but it was there nevertheless and made its presence felt when Ryder started moving suitcases around. When Anna began to cough she was immediately expelled, protesting, into the corridor outside.

'Go downstairs and wait,' ordered Ryder, with such consternation in his eyes that Anna gave in. 'If I find anything belonging to Ned I'll bring it down to the kitchen.'

'You don't have to do this, Ryder,' she gasped.

'I might as well now I've started, but only if you get out of here right away,' he said relentlessly. 'Now, Anna.'

'I'm going, I'm going!'

When Anna reached the kitchen she went straight outside to take a few deep breaths of cold, dust-free air, then went inside again to fill a glass with water and drank it down, feeling guilty. Searching through a dusty attic was probably the last thing Ryder needed right now. Anna prowled around the room as she waited, on fire with impatience by the time Ryder came in with a battered leather suitcase.

'You found it!' she said, delighted.

'It's locked, and God knows where the keys are,' he announced, 'but before I operate on it I need a shower. I'm filthy.'

'The suitcase is pretty grubby too. If you put it down in the scullery I'll get it cleaned up by the time you come back.'

Anna opened a few cupboard doors before she found the dust cloths she wanted, plus newspapers in a neat pile, ready for recycling. She cleaned the suitcase thoroughly, then spread a layer of newspaper on the kitchen table and laid the suitcase on top. She eyed it without much hope as she washed her hands in the sink. The case was so easy to handle there was probably nothing inside it.

Ryder came hurrying back with a screwdriver, rubbing his damp curls with a towel. He smiled when he saw the suitcase sitting on a bed of newspaper. 'Good girl. Martha wouldn't appreciate a mess on her table.' He applied the screwdriver to the clasps and grinned at Anna's excitement when they flew open.

When Ryder raised the lid Anna gazed down in disappointment at the neatly laundered khaki shirts, layered with bags of long-dry lavender. There was a well-worn leather case of shaving tackle and another containing hairbrushes, which gave out the faintest hint of bay rum, but no letters. Ryder shrugged. 'That's it. His uniform and boots and so on must be in one of the trunks. His medal hangs in a frame under his portrait.'

'You've got a portrait of him?' Anna's eyes lit up.

'Come upstairs and I'll introduce you. I'll take the suitcase back at the same time.'

Ryder put the suitcase down when they reached the landing and pointed to two photographs on the wall near the head of the stairs. Two young men smiled from oval frames, both in army officer's uniform. They had curling dark hair and, even though the portraits were in monochrome, their black-fringed eyes were obviously as blue as Ryder's. The framed Military Cross suspended from one of the frames told Anna she was looking at Captain Edward Wyndham.

His eyes looked tired and his face was too haggard for one so young, but the charm of his wry smile was powerful.

'Wow,' said Anna softly. 'Just look at him—the answer to every maiden's prayer. Violet never stood a chance.'

Ryder put the suitcase down and slid his arm round her waist. 'How about his brother George—the one who made it home? The likeness is pretty strong.'

She shook her head, unable to tear her eyes away. 'Edward's face has a world-weariness the other face lacks—totally irresistible.'

'I'm getting jealous of my own great-uncle,' said Ryder in disgust and Anna stood on tiptoe to kiss him.

'You're irresistible too, Ryder Wyndham.'

'In that case…' He picked her up suddenly, ignoring the suitcase, which went careering down the stairs. 'Time for my reward.'

Ryder's bedroom looked out over the gardens to the farm land beyond, but Anna was given no time to look at the view. He laid her on the bed and leaned over her, kissing her as he undressed her. He released her hair from its clasp and ran his fingers through the long amber strands, smiling down into her eyes. 'So, fair maiden, I've got you where I want you at last.'

'You've still got your clothes on,' she pointed out breathlessly.

'Not for long.' He stripped off his clothes and joined her, uttering a savouring sound of pure pleasure as she pulled him against her. 'Skin on skin.' He rubbed his cheek against hers. 'Will you hit me if I ask a question?'

'It depends on the question.'

'If there's been no man in your life for a while, why do you still take contraceptive pills? And are you going to hit me because I asked?'

'No. In his job my father deals with a lot of young girls with unwanted pregnancies. So I take the pills and Dad sleeps a little easier.'

'I can see his point.' Ryder shook his head. 'Fatherhood is a pretty tough job.'

'Motherhood, too,' she said breathlessly, as his hands commenced a leisurely, importuning progress over those parts of her body which sprang into quivering life at his touch. 'Ryder…'

He licked his tongue over her lips. 'Whatever you want, the answer's yes.'

She chuckled. 'You'll regret saying that one day. Are you going to make love to me every time we meet?'

'Of course I am.' Ryder moved over her, balancing on his elbows to smile down at her. 'We've got a lot of time to make up. And I need memories to store up for the time when you're miles away in London. In the meantime—'

'Let's make love!'

'You read my mind.'

She caressed the long, muscular back with inciting hands as Ryder kissed her until they were both breathless, their hearts hammering against each other. But Anna stiffened when Ryder slid down, trailing fire along her body with his seeking, caressing tongue. When it penetrated between her thighs she gave a startled gasp as his tongue met its target like a heat-seeking missile. She tried to push his head away, but he held her hands in one of his and brought her to the very brink before sliding up over her and into her, his face buried in her hair as they moved together in mounting frenzy towards the moment of glory Anna experienced in time to clutch Ryder close in possessive arms as he shuddered in the throes of his own climax.

The twilight faded into darkness in the quiet room as their breathing slowed. 'I hated that, before,' said Anna, in a voice she hardly recognised as her own.

'Before what?'

'Before making love with you.'

'If you didn't like it, I could promise not to do it again.'

She thought about it. 'I suppose it would be interesting to experience it once more—to find out why it's different with you.'

'It's different with me,' said Ryder, turning her in his arms, 'because you belong to me. And I belong to you. We were soul mates when we were young, Anna, and, in spite of everything that's happened in our lives since, that's never changed. We've merely added a new element to the mix.'

'A very powerful element,' she said drowsily and curled up against him.

Ryder held Anna close as she drifted into sleep, shaken by the strength of his feelings for her. At Oxford he'd met a lot of clever, pretty girls and enjoyed the experience to the full. And in his working life in the City he'd met a lot more only too happy to take advantage of everything he had to offer. Some of them had shown signs of wanting a more permanent relationship, but he'd never been the least tempted to ask one of them to share his life, least of all Edwina, who'd reeled him in with the oldest trick in the book. But at last, right here in his arms, he had a woman who felt utterly right there.

After a few minutes Anna stirred against him and raised her head to smile sleepily in apology. 'Sorry. I was so comfortable I dozed off.'

He kissed her nose. 'I'm not complaining. In fact, why don't you lie there while I go down and forage for something to eat?'

Anna shot upright in contrition. 'Ryder, I feel terrible! Mrs Carter asked me to sort supper for you and I forgot.'

Ryder laughed and held her close. 'You gave me something I'll take in preference to food any day—or night.'

She rubbed her cheek against his. 'I'll keep that in mind. But if you'll just let me go right now we'll go foraging together. I'm hungry.'

He slid out of bed and pulled Anna with him, laughing when she raced to pick up her clothes the moment her feet hit the ground.

'Turn your back while I get dressed,' she ordered.

'Not a chance. I want to watch.'

Anna shook her head vehemently, clutching her clothes to her chest. 'No.'

His eyes danced. 'Why not? I undressed you.'

'That's different.'

'Why?'

'I'm not used to you in this way yet. I can't let you watch me in cold blood!'

'My blood is anything but cold.'

'Ryder,' she said in desperation. *'Please.'*

He raised a hand in laughing surrender and turned away to dress. Anna scrambled hurriedly into her clothes at top speed, embarrassed over making a fuss. Making love with Ryder was doing damage to her brain cells.

'Can I turn round now?' demanded Ryder, and she began to laugh.

'Yes. Sorry I was an idiot.'

He turned to take her hand. 'You're insulting the woman I love. Come on, let's find something to eat.'

When they reached the head of the stairs Anna exclaimed in distress. The suitcase lay open on the curve of the staircase below, its contents strewn around it. Ryder ran down to gather them up and Anna hurried after him to fold the shirts he handed her. She was so intent on trying to return them to the original creases that she didn't notice Ryder's silence as he gazed down into the suitcase.

'Darling,' he said softly, holding out his hand, 'come here.'

Anna got up to take his hand, her heart thumping when she saw that the fall had dislodged a false bottom to the suitcase. Ryder tugged it out and picked up the cracked leather folder that lay beneath.

'Let's sit down,' Anna whispered.

Ryder drew her down beside him, putting his arm round her as she touched the stained leather with a questing finger. 'Go on—open it, Anna.'

Her hands shook with excitement as she took out the photograph inside. A romantic sepia study by a London photographer showed a shyly smiling girl with fair hair piled on top of her head and a posy of violets on a ribbon round her slender bare throat.

'Miss Violet Hodge, no doubt,' said Ryder huskily and turned the photograph over. On the back, in girlish looping handwriting, the sitter had written: 'To my dearest Ned, with all my love forever, Violet.'

Anna sniffed unashamedly. 'She's so *young*.'

'And so beautiful,' said Ryder. 'The letters under the flap are obviously hers.' He took the folder and hauled Anna to her feet. 'Let's read them in the kitchen over that supper you forgot.'

Anna put a salad together to accompany the savoury tart Martha had left for them, but insisted the letters wait until after supper.

'You could light a fire in the morning room while I clear away,' she suggested as they sat down to eat.

'You want to stay here for the evening?' Ryder asked, surprised. 'I thought I'd hitch a ride to Keeper's with you and walk back later on. Much later on.'

'Much as I love my cottage, I'd enjoy an hour or two here with you before I go back to it.' She smiled. 'No one will see my car parked outside *your* door.'

'You can park your car outside my door any time you like,' he assured her.

When they were in front of a crackling fire in the morning room later, Ryder smoothed out the letters from the folder and drew Anna close as they began to read. Violet's love for Ned poured from the page as she told him how much she missed him and how she prayed for him morning and night. She related anecdotes about the infants she taught in the village school and gave him snippets of local news, but the last letter contained news Violet had obviously found so hard to write that there were tearstains on the page. She wrote that she was now sure she was expecting his baby in the autumn, a sequel to the bliss of the stolen week spent together in London on his last leave. She assured him she was happy about this and hoped and prayed that he would be too.

There was one more letter, half-finished, but this was from Ned to Violet, telling her that he was delighted about the baby, loved her more than ever and they would be married as soon as he got leave.

'But, before he could get it off to her, he was killed,' said Ryder quietly.

'And he left Violet grieving for him, never knowing that he knew about the baby, let alone that he was delighted about it.' Anna sighed. 'Marriage to someone else was her only option. I hope James Bloxham was kind to her.'

'He wasn't required to make the effort for long. Violet and her baby son were dead before the year was out.' Ryder got up and pulled Anna to her feet. 'Let's put Ned's letters in the writing case with Violet's and put everything back where we found it.'

Anna nodded, tears clinging to her eyelashes. 'They'll be together at last.'

Ryder fetched the suitcase and put the folder in first, then secured the false bottom in place. Anna laid everything neatly on top and Ryder closed the lid and snapped the clasps into place. 'Stay here by the fire while I take it back.'

When she was alone Anna poked the fire and put another log on it, then stood gazing at the leaping flames until Ryder came back. He took her hand and led her back to the sofa to settle her beside him, close in his arms. They sat there together for the rest of the evening, content just to savour the reality of being alive and together, all the heat and passion of earlier transmuted into basic pleasure in each other's company. But when it grew late Anna insisted she drive home alone, rather than have Ryder face a walk back in the rain driving against the tall windows.

'Come to dinner tomorrow instead,' she said, and smiled up at him. 'This time I'll make you a proper meal and you can come in the Land Rover. I was joking about my reputation. I don't care who sees your car at my gate.'

'Progress!' said Ryder, but he frowned as they went out on to the portico together. 'Hell, it's coming down in stair-rods. Hold on, I'll get an umbrella.' When he got back he held it over her as she unlocked the car. 'For God's sake, drive carefully. And ring me the minute you get in.'

'I will.' She held up her face and Ryder kissed her hard, then held the door open for her to slide inside. She switched on the ignition, blew him a kiss and drove off. She took a peep into the mirror before turning down the drive and saw him standing there in the pouring rain, one hand raised until she was out of sight.

The following week passed all too quickly. Anna spent time with Mrs Jessop over the choice of colour and blooms for the flower arrangements and, with Ryder's permission, Anna told her she'd been right about Violet's letters and described their discovery over coffee while the vicar was at a parish council meeting. Otherwise Anna counted the hours until she could be with Ryder. Soon, she knew, it would be time to leave and get back to work, but for the moment she refused to think of the future. The present was all that mattered.

They spent Friday evening at Keeper's Cottage, in common with every other evening that week since Ryder flatly refused to let Anna drive home alone again. She had a more elaborate dinner than usual waiting for him, and they ate at the table with candles and wine and the china Hector had kept for special occasions. But as soon as the meal was over they went upstairs to bed, unable to wait a moment longer without making love. Afterwards they lay in each other's arms, talking endlessly, until at last Ryder heaved himself out of bed.

'I hate this part,' he said savagely as he pulled his clothes on. 'But, before I go, let's make some coffee and sit in the parlour. I've got something to say.'

Anna looked at him in alarm as she wrapped herself in her dressing gown. 'That sounds ominous. What is it?'

'Let's go downstairs first.'

Ryder refused to say another word until they were sitting in the parlour with cups of coffee in front of them, by which time Anna was on tenterhooks.

'For heaven's sake, Ryder, spit it out,' she ordered, annoyed to hear her voice crack.

'I've done a lot of hard thinking,' he said, taking her hand. 'Ned and Violet made it tragically plain how short life—and love—can be, so I've decided to come to the point rather sooner than I intended. These past few days have shown what an enormous help you could be to me, Anna.' His eyes fastened on hers. 'You're not overjoyed at the thought of going back to your job in London, but the very fact that you are an accountant means you could take over that part of my job and make sure I keep the taxman happy. And, on the plus side, we would be seeing each other on a daily basis.'

Anna raked a hand through her tumbled hair. 'This is all a bit sudden—'

'*Sudden!*' He let out a bark of mirthless laughter. 'We've known each other for twenty-five years, Anna.'

'On and off,' she reminded him. 'And mostly off. There were years when you forgot I even existed.'

He shook his head. 'I never forgot you. Ever. But you avoided me so successfully it was obvious you preferred to forget me. But things have changed—dramatically—between us these past few days. I see no point in wasting more time apart.'

'I'm not sure I know what you have in mind,' she said, hardly daring to hope.

'Don't worry. I'm well aware of your opinion about marriage and babies, so I'm not asking you to change your life to that extent.'

Mortified disappointment rendered Anna speechless for a moment. 'Let me get this straight,' she said at last. 'What exactly *do* you have in mind?'

'I want you to work for me, Anna. I could pay you a reasonable wage—'

'And of course I have a place to live,' she said coldly. 'It's a very convenient arrangement all round.'

'I would have asked you to move into the Manor with me, but I had an idea that wouldn't meet with your approval.' Ryder lounged back in his corner of the sofa, ankles crossed and looking so relaxed she wanted to hit him. But a tell-tale throb at the corner of his expressive mouth told her he was no more relaxed than she was.

Anna got up and went to the fireplace, then turned with sudden resolution to face him. 'Listen, Ryder. Your family has lived at the Manor for forever—'

'Not forever. Only since my great-great-grandfather made a packet in the food canning industry and had a fancy to become gentry,' he contradicted. 'He bought the house from the impoverished Squire of the time, and dubbed himself Squire from that day on. Forgive the interruption,' he added smoothly. 'You were saying?'

Ryder's social climbing ancestor was such news to Anna that she was thrown for a moment. 'I never knew that. But the fact remains—no matter how your family came by the house, Ryder, they've lived there a long time and the estate has been handed down from son to son ever since.' She looked at him squarely. 'Gramp told me that all Wyndham brides were expected to produce an heir and a spare at the very least.'

Ryder's eyes narrowed. 'And your point is?'

'You'll naturally want a bride some time to do the same. I've made my views very clear about children, so I'd rather end this now than get in the way when you find someone happy to provide them for you. The role of discarded mistress doesn't appeal.'

He sat very still, his face a handsome mask. 'You'd actually take off now and pretend none of this happened between us?'

'No, Ryder,' she said in desperation. 'I just want things to go on as they are.'

Ryder got up with such sudden violence that Anna backed away. 'You mean I should sneak over to this place for sex when you can spare the time from your job and your London life to drive down here.'

The silence which followed Ryder's angry pronouncement became so prolonged that Anna felt something shrivel up and die inside her.

'If that's the way you look at it, there's nothing more to say,' she said at last.

'On that, at least, we agree.' He gave her a mirthless smile. 'I'd better remove my well-known car from your gate and get home.' He waited for a moment, but when she said nothing he gave a negligent shrug. 'Goodbye, then, Anna. Take care of yourself.'

Anna waited for the front door to close behind him, but this time she stayed where she was instead of rushing to the window to watch as he walked down the path, in case she flung the door open and begged him to come back. If he did she knew she would throw herself into his arms to agree with anything he wanted, which would be a disaster. It was pointless to prolong the agony.

After she heard the car drive away, Anna rang her father but, to her infinite relief, his answering service was the only response. She left a message to cancel his visit to Keeper's Cottage and told him she was driving to Shrewsbury first thing in the morning instead to spend a few days at home before going back to work. She packed her clothes and went straight to bed, but Ryder's scent lingered on the sheets and, after tossing and turning all night, she gave up by five in the morning. At six she drove away from Keeper's Cottage, feeling as though she'd left part of herself there to haunt it.

CHAPTER TEN

ANNA had timed herself to arrive while her father was taking morning surgery. She scribbled a note to him and went straight up to her room to crawl into bed. But after a while her conscience prodded her to let Ryder know where she was. She sent him a text and tried to sleep, but eventually she gave up and checked her phone. There was no message from Ryder. There was none from him later that day either, nor on any other day during her stay with her father.

Not, Anna assured herself, that she'd expected a proposal of marriage from Ryder. With their different backgrounds it would never have worked for them. Ryder loved every stick and stone of Wyndham Manor, whereas she just couldn't imagine giving up her job and her life in London to make her home there. If Clare and Charlie Saunders, who had a lot more in common than most couples, couldn't make a go of marriage there was fat chance for Anna Morton and Ryder Wyndham. Not that a marriage offer had ever been on the table. No matter what he said about his social-climbing ancestor, Ryder was justifiably proud of his heritage and wanted an heir to carry on the name. So, no matter how much she loved him, it was best to make the break now before things went too far. Because she did love him, Anna admitted at last. She'd loved him since she was eight years old if she was counting.

* * *

Ryder had found life hard enough in the period following his brother's death, but after Anna left it sank into a black hole. Until meeting up with her again he'd hardly noticed he possessed a libido. Now, no matter how tired he was, he lay awake at night craving her, haunted by memories of making love to her in this same bed he tossed and turned on all night through. He'd been so sure that she loved him, and shared the unique rapport that was even stronger between them now they were lovers, and he'd fondly imagined his suggestion about a job was the best way to persuade her to stay here. But he'd been so far off the mark she'd taken off next morning, depriving him of not only a lover but a friend he valued above all others.

Ryder knew that Martha was deeply concerned about him, but she would never dream of asking what was troubling him, thank God. And, though Anna's sudden departure meant extra work for him with regard to the ball, he was glad of it. Or would be if he thought for a moment she'd turn up.

'You still look peaky,' remarked Clare, when Anna got home late as usual a few weeks later. 'I made a sort of stew thing and kept you some. No argument please; I insist that you eat it.'

Anna stifled a yawn. 'Thanks, Clare, but you needn't have bothered. I had a big lunch.'

Clare Saunders raised a cynical eyebrow. 'Your nose just grew an inch then, Anna Morton.'

Anna smiled sheepishly. 'Things are hectic right now.'

'I know that. And because I'm a warm, understanding kind of woman I will let you have a shower first, but then I insist that you eat.' Clare fixed her with a relentless green eye. 'I do not want to start visiting you in that hospital again.'

Anna threw up her hands in surrender. 'Give me twenty minutes.' She turned as she went into her room. 'Any messages?'

'No, darling.'

Anna wondered why she still bothered to ask. Everyone she knew used a mobile phone anyway. But there was always the outside chance that Ryder might have rung the flat instead. Hope persisted even after it became depressingly obvious that this wasn't going to happen. If any overtures were to be made she would have to make them. And, since that wasn't going to happen either, it was time to stop hoping and face facts. Her brief, blazing interlude with Ryder was over. And whoever said it was better to have loved and lost was talking rubbish. If she hadn't found out what love could really be like between a man and a woman she might have more success in sleeping at night. By love, of course, she meant sex. Only that wasn't true, either. Making love with Ryder was a lot more than just glorious, heart-stopping sex. It was warmth and closeness and belonging, and without him she felt as though part of her was missing. She sighed despondently. Just to be in the same room with him and breathe the same air would be enough right now. So all she had to do was pick up a phone and say she'd changed her mind, that she'd do whatever he wanted as long as they still kept seeing each other. But even as the thought formed she went cold, the towel clutched to her breasts as she pictured Ryder looking down his Wyndham nose as he told her he'd changed *his* mind.

When Anna sat down to eat, the aroma of Clare's savoury stew was so tempting her taste buds perked up and she gratified the chef by eating everything in her bowl and mopping it out with bread afterwards.

'Thanks, Clare,' she said fervently as she sat back. 'That was delicious—just what I needed.'

'Actually you're lucky it survived. Charlie called in earlier and showed me how to make the dumplings, but I wouldn't let him stay to supper so he went off in a huff.'

'Poor Charlie.'

'He can make his own supper. He's a much better cook than I am.' Clare put a small carton down in front of Anna. 'Supermarket trifle for pudding.'

'You shouldn't be doing all this! You're just as busy as me.'

'I promised your father I'd make sure you ate properly.'

'I'll make dinner tomorrow night,' offered Anna, conscience-stricken.

Clare shook her head, smiling. 'No need. Charlie's feeding me at his place. But there's some stew left and it's always better the following day, so promise me you'll finish it off.'

Since the stew was delicious and the promise involved nothing more strenuous than switching on a microwave, Anna made it gladly. 'Are you staying over at Charlie's tomorrow?'

'I might.' Clare's eyes glinted wickedly. 'There are three things my darling ex is very good at. He's a first-rate journalist and a pretty good chef. I leave the third to your imagination.'

Since her recent experience with Ryder, Anna's imagination could picture it only too vividly. 'In that case why couldn't you stay married?'

'I've told you before, darling. Day to day domesticity was hard for both of us. Our relationship works much better this way.'

With intense concentration Anna scraped the last of the trifle from the carton and licked the spoon. 'Clare, as a matter of interest, which do you like best? Going out with Charlie or a night in just talking together?'

Her friend looked at her sharply. 'Why do you ask?'

'I just wondered.'

'I enjoy both. We're in the same line of work so we always have loads to talk about.' Clare paused, her eyes troubled. 'Anna, you've changed since you came back. Your physical health has obviously improved, but otherwise you really worry me. Are you still grieving for Hector?'

'I am, of course, but it's easing slowly.'

Clare looked doubtful. 'If you say so. When are you going to the cottage again?'

'Not any time soon,' Anna assured her. 'At the moment I need lazy weekends to get over my working week.'

'Don't think I haven't noticed. Are you taking all the vitamins you should be taking?'

'Yes, Mother!'

Clare grinned as she went over to her desk. 'I forgot. A very posh letter came for you today.'

Anna tensed as she opened a thick white envelope which contained a familiar embossed card with gilt edges. It was the invitation to the ball, her name written in Ryder's unmistakable handwriting, but with no added note coaxing her to turn up. Not that she'd expected one, of course. But she'd hoped.

Clare raised an eyebrow as she read it. 'Very fancy. Are you going?'

'I don't know.'

Clare shot Anna a searching look. 'It's just occurred to me that you've talked a lot about the burglary, but very little about Ryder, except that he put you up that night. I hope you kissed and made up?'

'More or less. Life's too short to stay hostile for long.'

'Good thinking.' Clare smiled wickedly. 'If I had a childhood pal like Ryder Wyndham I wouldn't be hostile in the first place. That man is seriously mouth-watering—' She stared in horror as Anna burst into tears. 'Oh, darling, what have I said? What's wrong?'

After weeks of keeping her troubles close to her chest, Anna suddenly lost it. She buried her face in her hands as the dam burst and, between tearing sobs, told her friend most of what really happened during her time at Keeper's Cottage. Clare patted her shoulder until Anna showed signs of drying out, then got up to make coffee.

'You need caffeine,' she said firmly.

'When I was upset over the break-in Ryder made me hot chocolate,' said Anna thickly, mopping her face.

'That man's just too perfect to live. Seriously though, Anna, I'm at a loss here. Ryder's the playmate you hero-worshipped when you were young; he went riding to the rescue when you were burgled, and I can't believe he's not a terrific lover. So why have you quarrelled?'

'Children.'

'Ah.' The intelligent green eyes narrowed. 'Any reason why you can't produce some?'

'Nothing physical.' Anna eyed her friend ruefully. 'I feel like a total freak for admitting it, but strictly between you and me, Clare, I just don't want any. The very thought of motherhood scares me rigid.'

'I can understand that. I feel the same. But at least Charlie was in complete agreement. Ryder would like a son to carry on the Wyndham name, of course.'

'More than one, probably. Wyndham brides are expected to produce the obligatory heir and a spare.' Anna smiled damply. 'Ryder's mother went one better than that, but took so long about producing her third son, Dominic calls himself The Accident.'

Clare smiled. 'I only met him for a moment, but young Dominic struck me as quite a lad.'

'Oddly enough, that's how the vicar's wife described Ryder in his wilder days. Nothing more irresistible than a reformed rake, according to Mrs Jessop.'

Clare handed Anna a mug. 'And is he irresistible?'

'Totally. So I removed myself from temptation and left him free to find someone who will give him children.'

'How about the ball? Will you go?'

'Dad and Tom will have received invitations too, so, short of being whisked off to hospital again, I can't see myself getting out of it.' Anna shivered. 'But in the circumstances I'm not looking forward to it much.'

'With such stalwart double protection you'll be fine,' said Clare firmly. 'When do we go shopping for a dress?'

But Anna couldn't bring herself to think of shopping for a while. Her life seemed to consist of work and bed and no play at all except for the Saturday evening when her father and Tom travelled up to the flat for a meal which Charlie Saunders helped Clare and Anna produce. The result was a highly entertaining evening and a cordon bleu dinner, and afterwards Clare went home with Charlie to give the Mortons time together over break-fast the next morning.

'You've had your invitation to the ball, of course, Cinderella?' said Tom, tucking into the vast plateful Anna had cooked for him.

'Of course,' she said loftily.

'Have you spoken to Ryder since you came back to London?' asked her father casually.

'No. Why?'

'I just wondered.'

'You were so frosty towards him at the funeral, you're damn lucky he bothered to help out when you had the break-in,' said Tom bluntly. 'Did the burglary put you off staying at the cottage alone? You haven't been back there since.'

'I just haven't had time, but I'll be there for the big event.' Anna poured coffee and sat down, smiling sweetly. 'I assume you gentlemen will be my guests?'

John Morton laughed. 'I rather took that for granted. Should we pay you for our room and board?'

'That's a thought,' said Tom soberly.

'No charge for family,' Anna assured him.

John smiled. 'Remember how excited you were about the dress you had for Ryder's eighteenth birthday party?'

As if she could ever forget.

'I missed out on that,' said Tom in disgust. 'I had chicken-pox. At that age! You sent Anna off to Gramp out of the way, Dad.'

'But she didn't stay long. Father brought her back straight after the party, worried that she was coming down with the same thing, but it was a false alarm.'

'Right,' said Anna briskly, getting up. 'Are you two staying to lunch?'

To her surprise, both her men looked rather sheepish as they declined.

'Not me, I must get back,' said John Morton. 'Medical dinner,' he said vaguely.

Anna eyed him narrowly. On a Sunday night?

'I've got a medical dinner too, of a kind,' said Tom with relish. 'Our new anaesthetist is entertaining me tonight.'

'He or she?' said Anna, fluttering her eyelashes. 'And, if the latter, does the entertainment involve food?'

'*She,*' said Tom loftily, 'is cooking her signature dish for me.'

'What is it?' asked his father, amused.

'Don't know, don't care.' Tom rolled his dark Morton eyes. 'If you met her you'd see why!'

Anna drove to Keeper's Cottage the following week in very different weather conditions from her previous visit. The sun was setting in a blaze of glory as she turned off into the Marches and this time she drove along the narrow, undulating roads with windows rolled down to let in the heady scent of newly cut grass. Spring had arrived with a bang in Little Over. The scent of cut grass was even stronger when Anna parked outside the cottage. The lawn had recently been mowed and the flower beds neatly weeded. She exhaled slowly. The Squire had certainly kept his promise to look after the property. Coals of fire, Ryder, she conceded.

Anna unlocked the door and switched off the alarm, then went straight upstairs to hang up the evening gown acquired on the shopping trip with Clare the previous weekend. She went back to the car for the rest and tensed when she saw a familiar Land Rover coming along the lane, then pinned a bright smile on her face to cover her disappointment. The man at the wheel had black curling hair and blue eyes but he was the wrong Wyndham.

'Hi there, Dominic,' she said cheerfully. 'How are you?'

He jumped down and gave her a hug. 'I'm good, Anna. But how are you? I heard about the pneumonia. What rotten luck!'

'I'm fine now. How are things shaping up for your big day?'

'Frankly I'll be glad when it finally arrives. The flight over yesterday was the first time in weeks I've had my bride to myself for a few hours.' Dominic rolled his eyes. 'Take my advice, Anna, when you get hitched take off to a register office and tell everyone afterwards.'

'I'll keep it in mind,' she said dryly.

'I was very sorry to hear about your grandfather,' he said, suddenly grave. 'I shall miss him.'

Anna sighed. 'Me too.'

'Ryder says he left the cottage to you.'

'Yes. Though I don't get much chance to come down here.'

'Boyfriends keeping you busy in London?'

'Fat chance. The fiscal year took up all my time until recently. How is Hannah?'

'Excited. I've told her all about you, so she's dying to meet you on Saturday. Hannah's family flew over with us. Ryder's showing my in-laws round the estate as we speak, so I volunteered to run some errands for Martha.' Dominic rubbed his nose, eyeing her quizzically. 'You were down here for a while after the funeral, Anna, so would you happen to know what's eating Ryder?'

She shook her head. 'No use asking me, Dominic.'

'He should hire a new estate manager. He's working too hard.'

She shivered. 'It's a bit chilly out here; do you want to come in? I can rustle up a glass of wine.'

'Love to, Anna, but I must get back or I'll have Martha after me. Ryder asked me to call in on my way past and see if you needed anything.'

She blinked. 'How did he know I was coming today?'

'Tom told him.' Dominic picked up her suitcases. 'I'll just carry these in for you before I take off.'

Anna looked at him questioningly as they walked up the path. 'Would you happen to know who did my garden?'

'Ryder probably sent over one of Bob Godfrey's lads. They've done a marvellous job on the grounds at the Manor.' He laughed. 'You should see the marquee Ryder ordered.'

'I will, tomorrow.' She smiled at him. 'Nice to see you, Dominic. And thank Ryder for sorting the garden for me.'

'Thank him yourself tomorrow,' he said promptly, then looked at his watch and pulled a face. 'Time I was off. Great to see you, Anna.' He gave her another hug, then took off at a run.

Anna closed the door, put her bags of groceries in the kitchen, then sent a message to Clare to say she'd arrived, wishing now that she'd faked a relapse to avoid the ball. But with two doctors in the family that was too tricky to pull off. She took the cases upstairs and unpacked clothes from one and bed linen from the other, made up the beds and went downstairs to wait for her father and Tom. They arrived within minutes of each other and once the three of them began catching up with each other's news Anna began to feel she might possibly enjoy the weekend after all. As she poured coffee she asked approval of the dinner menu she'd planned for later.

'You can put your chef's hat away, love,' Tom said, smiling smugly. 'I've booked a table at the Red Lion tonight.'

Anna dressed with care later, just in case—in case what? she thought irritably. She was unlikely to run into Ryder the night before the ball. Nevertheless she dressed in a clinging silk jersey shift the colour of bitter chocolate and eyed herself critically in the long glass lining her wardrobe door. Not bad. No one would be able to tell that her heart was heavy under her fine feathers.

'You look delicious, Anna. Is that dress new?' asked John Morton as she went downstairs.

'No, I've had it for ages. I say, Tom,' she added as her brother ran down to join them in a fawn needlecord suit, 'did you buy that to wow your lady anaesthetist?'

'I did, and it did. Her name's Rachel,' he informed her, then whistled in surprise when John Morton opened a bottle of champagne to fill the three glasses waiting on the table in the parlour. 'What are we celebrating, Dad?' he asked.

'The news I'm about to spring on you,' announced John Morton, smiling wryly. 'I'm getting married again. I hadn't screwed up enough courage to propose to Nancy when you were at home with me, Anna, but I finally popped the question a couple of days ago and she said yes, so will you both wish me happy?'

'Oh, Dad,' said Anna, and threw her arms round him. 'Of course we will—' She stopped dead, her eyes widening. 'Nancy? Do you mean Grace's mother?'

Grace Todd had been Anna's friend since primary school, second only to Ryder in the friendship pecking order. Anna had been bridesmaid at Grace's wedding, godmother to her baby boy, and all three Mortons had provided support at the funeral of Grace's father a few years earlier.

'That's great news, Dad,' said Tom warmly and hugged his father. 'I suppose you were giving Mrs Todd time to get over her loss.'

'Too much time, apparently,' said John ruefully. 'When I finally risked proposing, guess what she said.'

'She thought you'd never ask!' said Anna, laughing.

The Red Lion chef was gifted and the conversation was animated over dinner as the three Mortons talked wedding plans. They stayed at the table to drink coffee afterwards, but when they left the dining room Anna went suddenly quiet as a tall, familiar figure intercepted them, visible marks of fatigue below his spectacular blue eyes.

'I called in to check on a booking for some friends for tomorrow night,' said Ryder after the greetings were over. 'I was told you were here tonight, Doctor. How are you?'

'Very well.' John Morton smiled at him warmly. 'I'm glad of the chance to give you my personal thanks for helping Anna when the cottage was burgled.'

'I was only too happy to help,' said Ryder. 'How are you feeling, Anna?'

'Absolutely fine,' she said brightly.

'I'm glad.' He turned to Tom. 'I'm still waiting for you to make that fishing trip.'

'I've had other fish to fry lately,' said Tom, grinning. 'I'll bring Rachel down to meet you one day. How about you, Ryder? Still fancy-free?'

'If you're asking if I have a new woman in my life, the answer's no.' The dark-ringed eyes turned on Anna. 'How about your life?'

'Just work in mine,' she said coolly.

'Nothing new, then.'

Tom glanced at the two set faces, then excused himself to pay the bill.

'Hold on, Tom,' said his father. 'Let me pay it.'

While the Mortons wrangled over the bill, Ryder moved closer to Anna. 'You look beautiful.'

'Thanks. You look tired.'

He gave her a long, unsmiling look. 'I don't sleep well these days.'

She felt herself flush. 'Thank you so much for having my garden sorted. I wasn't expecting that. You must tell me how much I owe you.'

'Nothing at all. I told you I'd keep an eye on it,' he reminded her.

'It was very good of you, Ryder,' said John Morton as he came back with Tom.

'I'm only too glad to help.'

'By the way, Ryder,' said Tom. 'I'm sure my father won't mind if I give you his news. Dad's just informed us he's getting married soon.'

Ryder smiled warmly. 'My sincere congratulations, Doctor.'

'I'm a fortunate man,' agreed John.

'In more ways than one,' said Anna brightly. 'Nancy's cooking is legendary.'

Her father smiled. 'I admit I look forward to going home to her meals instead of my own efforts. But I wouldn't really care if Nancy couldn't boil an egg. I just want her to share my life.'

'I can understand that, Doctor,' said Ryder quietly.

John Morton looked stricken for a moment. 'I'm a tactless idiot—I'm sorry.'

'If you mean Edwina, don't be,' Ryder assured him and apologised, embarrassed, as a yawn defeated him.

'Speaking professionally,' said John Morton kindly, 'it might be a good idea if you went home and got some sleep. In fact it's time we all got to bed.'

'You're right, sir,' said Ryder. 'The caterers are due at some ungodly hour in the morning and the rest of my house guests will probably turn up straight after breakfast.' He held Anna back behind the others as they went outside to the car park. 'When do you go back to London?'

'Sunday afternoon.'

'I want to talk to you before you go. Ring me after Tom and your father leave and I'll come over.'

She nodded silently and caught up with the others to link arms with her father. 'It's a fine night. It looks as though the sun will shine on your party tomorrow, Ryder.'

He gave her a sardonic smile. 'It always does on the righteous! I'll see you all tomorrow. Goodnight.'

'I know the ball is an introduction to Dominic's bride,' said John Morton on the way back to Keeper's, 'but isn't he rather young to be getting married?'

'Hannah works in the porcelain department in the same auction house,' said Tom. 'Ryder says they're well suited.'

'You seem to be in contact with Ryder quite a lot,' commented his father.

'He's been ringing me more than usual lately,' admitted Tom and gave Anna a sidelong glance. 'But he takes far more interest in my sister's welfare than mine—always has.'

Anna woke next morning to sunshine, threw on a dressing gown and ran downstairs to find her father drinking tea in front of the television.

'Good morning, darling,' he said, smiling. 'You were right about the weather. The forecast says settled and sunny for this part of the world.'

'Excellent news for my dress!' She bent to kiss him. 'Sorry I'm late, Dad. I meant to be down early to get the breakfast started.'

'You don't have to cook for us, Anna. I foraged for myself, and Tom can do the same when he surfaces.' He followed her to the kitchen, giving her a professional scrutiny. 'You're still too thin.'

'I'll soon pile on the pounds now things are slowing down at work.' Anna smiled at him as she filled the kettle. 'It's wonderful news about your wedding. I'm really glad for you, Dad.'

'You don't mind having a stepmother?'

'Not this one! Nancy's been like a mother to me for years, anyway. I bet Grace is tickled pink about having you for a stepfather too.'

'She assures me that she is.' John smiled. 'She gave me a message for you, by the way. Your services as godmother will be required again soon.'

Anna's eyebrows rose as she put a slice of bread in the toaster. 'That's a bit quick off the mark. My godson is barely past his first birthday.'

'Grace says she can't afford to hang about at her age.' John bit his lip as Anna winced. 'I know she's the same age as you, darling, but women find fulfilment in different ways. Grace prefers full-time motherhood to teaching, and you prefer a career.'

Anna buttered her toast with concentration. 'Would you have liked grandchildren, Dad?'

'Yes,' said her father honestly. 'But if neither you nor Tom oblige, I'll spoil Nancy's instead.'

CHAPTER ELEVEN

LATER that evening the Morton men were ready in formal dinner jackets talking medical shop and waiting patiently for Anna. When she finally appeared in strapless copper silk shot with gold, her hair in a mane of tousled curls, Tom gave a low whistle as she struck a pose.

'Wow! Great dress. Sexy hair too.'

'I'm glad you think so. It took hours! What do you think, Dad?' She did a twirl, holding out her sweeping skirt. 'Clare said this colour looks good with my hair.'

'She's right. You're an absolute picture.' He smiled lovingly, then tapped his watch. 'We'd better get going. We're late.'

'All the better to make a grand entrance,' said Tom, grinning. 'You'd better sit on your own in the back of the car, Cinderella, so we don't crease your dress.'

As her brother drove along the floodlit drive and through the gatehouse into the vast front courtyard Anna felt a great surge of nervous anticipation as she thought of the last time she'd come to the Manor for a party. But tonight she had two handsome escorts, her dress had a famous label and she knew she looked good. One of the young gardeners came to take Tom's keys to park the car as John Morton helped his daughter out and Anna picked up her rustling skirts to mount the steps under the main portico, her breath catching when Ryder came to meet them, tall and formidably good-looking in his sober black and white.

'Good evening, everyone.'

'Sorry we're a bit late, Ryder. Anna took a long time to get ready,' said Tom, grinning.

'The wait was more than worthwhile,' said Ryder smoothly, giving Anna a comprehensive survey. 'You look quite breathtaking tonight, Miss Morton.'

'Thank you,' she said with composure which faltered slightly when he bent to kiss her on both cheeks.

Ryder shook hands with her father and brother, then motioned them inside into the laughter and animated conversation in the packed entrance hall, which looked festive with the great chandelier shining down on a striking arrangement of flowers in the great urn at the foot of the stairs. Dominic immediately came hurrying towards them, towing a smiling girl by the hand, and after signalling a waiter to provide the Mortons with champagne, Ryder excused himself to return to his duties as host.

Hannah Breckenridge had long straight chestnut hair, a smattering of freckles across her nose and laughing grey eyes in a pointed face which was appealing rather than pretty. And, instead of the pin-thin figure Anna had pictured, there were rounded curves in all the right places under her apple-green satin gown.

'Anna, Dr Morton, Tom,' said Dominic, 'allow me to present Miss Hannah Breckenridge, soon to be Mrs Dominic Wyndham.'

'Doesn't that sound great?' Hannah held out her hand, her face glowing. 'It's so wonderful to meet all of you. But Dominic forgot to tell me you were drop dead gorgeous, Anna!'

'Why, thank you.' Anna felt herself flush.

'You're rather gorgeous yourself,' said John Morton gallantly.

Hannah smiled radiantly. 'How sweet of you to say so. And you're the other Dr Morton?' she said to Tom.

'Actually, he's a surgeon,' Dominic informed her. 'So he's known as Mr Morton.'

'But not to you, Hannah,' said Tom swiftly. 'I hope you'll save me a dance later.'

She smiled radiantly. 'I certainly will! Dominic says you

came here a lot when you were young. Isn't this the most fantastic house?'

'It certainly is,' agreed Anna.

'Just look at these flowers. Ryder said it was your idea to ask the vicar's wife to do them.' Hannah kept hold of Anna's hand as she called her parents over to meet the Mortons. Lois Breckenridge, brunette and elegant in slender midnight blue with diamonds, and her husband, Hartley, tall and affable with white streaks in hair like his daughter's, were friendly outgoing people, delighted to meet the family their daughter's fiancé had known all his life.

A red-coated master of ceremonies appeared soon afterwards to announce that dinner was served and the guests were directed outside to the marquee. It was a huge fairy-tale affair with glittering chandeliers, stars on the ceiling and flowers woven into ribbons garlanded round the supports to look like maypoles and in shallow, subtle arrangements on the tables arranged in one half of the marquee. A dance floor occupied the other half, with a small dais where a pianist was playing muted Gershwin standards. It was all a far cry from the occasion Anna remembered only too clearly from last time.

Once the guests were seated Oliver Jessop said grace, the first course was served and the man on Anna's right introduced himself as Troy Breckenridge, Hannah's older brother.

'I'm a committed Anglophile,' he told her. 'I was a Yank at Oxford and had the privilege of rowing in the Oxford/Cambridge boat race—great experience. Do you live here in the neighbourhood?'

Anna told him she was London-based, but that most of her school holidays had been spent running wild on the Wyndham Estate. 'My grandfather was head gamekeeper here,' she added, to Troy's frank delight.

'How British is that? This is such a great place. I envy Ryder Wyndham,' he informed her, and glanced over at Tom. 'Is that your husband?'

She shook her head. 'My brother.'

Troy gave Anna a wry grin. 'Just checking. I'd hate to tread on any toes, though I probably will later on the dance floor. Is there any other man I should know about?'

'Not a soul,' she said firmly.

'That's hard to believe!'

Anna laughed and took a sip from her glass, then looked up to meet such a cold blue look from Ryder at a neighbouring table that she flushed and turned to Dick Hammond on her right. 'How are the puppies coming along?'

Ryder had been seething with frustration as he watched Hannah's brother pay such practised attention to Anna. Seized with the urge to knock Troy Breckenridge's perfect white teeth down his throat, he turned away sharply and found that Lois Breckenridge was smiling at him in amusement.

'My son seems totally fascinated by Anna,' she said lightly. 'Is she a very special friend of yours, Ryder?'

'Yes, indeed.' He pulled himself together and smiled at her. 'We've known each other since we were children. She often helped me keep an eye on Dominic to give his nanny a break. He was quite a handful when he was little.'

Lois glanced across at Dominic and leaned nearer. 'I think maybe he's still a handful now he's grown-up,' she said in an undertone.

Ryder smiled reassuringly. 'Have no worries, Lois. Wyndham men may let off steam when they're single, but once they find the right woman they take marriage very seriously.'

'So why aren't you married, Ryder?'

He answered curtly, 'I don't have time.'

The lavish meal proceeded without a hitch. When it ended Ryder made a polished speech to thank his guests for joining him to wish happiness to Dominic and his future bride, then after toasts were drunk the tables were cleared and the ladies retired to the house for repairs while the men gathered on the terrace or took a stroll in the grounds. Anna slipped round to the kitchen for a chat with Martha and her helpers and received much admiration for her dress along with the cup of tea she asked for. On her way back to the marquee afterwards, Anna felt a sense of unwelcome *déjà vu* when she met a woman wearing a white dress printed with unfortunate red peonies.

'Hello, there,' said Edwina French in the high-pitched drawl which had changed so little that Anna felt her hackles jump to attention. 'I noticed you earlier. You look so familiar. I'm sure we've met before.'

'We have, briefly, but it was years ago at Ryder's eighteenth.' Anna waited a beat, smiling sweetly. 'I'm Anna Morton, the gamekeeper's brat.'

Edwina blinked and gave an embarrassed little laugh, her colour high. 'Did I actually say that? Frightfully sorry. Teenagers are such monsters.'

And you haven't changed, thought Anna, riveting her smile in place.

'I knew I'd seen you before when you arrived with that gorgeous man. Is he your husband?' demanded Edwina.

'I came with two gorgeous men. The younger one is my brother Tom, taking a day off from the operating theatre. The other is my father, Dr John Morton. Oh, look, here's *your* father coming to find you,' added Anna as Edwina's elderly, rotund escort came into view.

'Lawrence is my fiancé, actually,' said Edwina stiffly. 'He's looking for me—must dash.'

'Who was that?' demanded Tom as he joined her.

'The one and only Edwina French.'

'No!' He gazed after the ill-matched couple with interest. 'She's good-looking, I grant you, but not someone you'd want to cuddle up to. How the devil did she manage to catch Ryder?'

Anna shrugged. 'She lied about being pregnant.'

'Nice lady!'

When they got back to the table, a band had joined the

pianist and Troy Breckenridge was on his feet before Anna could sit down.

'May I have the pleasure?'

As they danced Troy asked questions about her career, told her about his own in the family firm and, when he discovered she'd never been to New York, he became persuasive.

'You'll be receiving an invitation to Hannah's wedding soon,' he informed her. 'You must be sure to come over for it, Anna. I'll take considerable pleasure in showing you round my home town.'

She smiled without committing herself as they returned to the table and Tom promptly got up and demanded the next dance.

'Unless it's a tango,' he warned.

'It's not a tango and it's not your dance, either, Morton—it's mine, and long overdue,' said Ryder as he joined them. He held out his hand to Anna. 'May I?'

She nodded, conscious of Troy Breckenridge's speculative eyes. 'I'm not very good at this,' she warned as they took the floor.

'You were doing well enough with Breckenridge,' he said tightly.

'He's a very good dancer.'

'With a good chat-up line, obviously. You were hanging on his every word.'

'He's a very interesting man. He wants me to go to New York for Dominic's wedding.'

Ryder held her closer, his hand sliding up to the bare skin above the bronze silk. 'I'm not surprised he wants to see you again, the way you look tonight, Anna.' He bent nearer. 'I wanted to ring you.'

'So why didn't you?'

'I was angry, hurt, shattered—all of the above. I had to cool down first. I decided to wait until I saw you again to say my piece, because it's better said face to face than on the phone.'

She looked up at him curiously. 'What is it?'

Ryder shook his head. 'Not here. I'll come over tomorrow.'

He sighed as the waltz came to an end. 'Duty calls. Save a dance for me later.'

'Is Edwina on your dance card?' Anna smiled evilly. 'We happened to meet earlier on. She said I looked familiar, so I took great pleasure in telling her I was the gamekeeper's brat. But I put my foot in it good and proper by referring to the large elderly gentleman as her father. Apparently he's her fiancé.'

Ryder let out a smothered crack of laughter. 'She must have loved that.' He let her go with reluctance as the music stopped. 'Thank you, Anna. I've waited a hell of a long time for that dance.' He turned as a hand fell on his shoulder and scowled at the thin, fair man grinning at him. 'I might have known it was you.'

'Toby Lonsdale!' exclaimed Anna in delight.

He made a sweeping bow. 'Anna Morton, all grown up and glorious! Will you dance with me?'

Dancing with Toby was such fun he insisted they stay on the floor for the entire set. They talked non-stop, reminiscing about the last time they'd danced together and filling in the gaps since. He told her that since becoming a barrister he specialised in divorce at chambers in Lincoln's Inn, had a divorce of his own under his belt, but was currently single. He looked impressed when Anna told him she hoped to be a partner at the accountancy firm she worked for.

'I wish I had such a beautiful accountant.' He glanced at her ringless left hand and raised a querying eyebrow.

She shook her head. 'Unattached, Toby.'

'Not for long, I think, darling. It's obvious to an old chum like me that Ryder wants to be a lot more than just your best friend these days. Trust me, I'm a lawyer!'

They laughed together as he took her back to the table and he kissed her cheek deliberately as Troy Breckenridge asked her to dance before she sat down.

'See you later,' said Toby as she was whisked away.

'I had to get in quickly,' said Troy, 'before some other guy ran off with you.' He gave her the wide white smile that Ryder objected to. 'You're the belle of the ball tonight, Miss Anna.'

'No way. That's your sister's role. Just look at her jiving with my brother over there—they're having enormous fun.'

'They certainly are,' he said, following her gaze. 'I sure hope Dominic's not the jealous type.'

'He won't be where Tom's concerned,' she said firmly. 'The Wyndhams and the Mortons were all children together.'

'Sounds idyllic.'

'It was. But, even as the best of friends do, we all grew up and went our different ways.' She smiled brightly. 'How long are you staying?'

'Long enough to see you again, I hope.'

She shook her head. 'I'm back in work on Monday.'

'Then let me take you to lunch tomorrow.'

'Sorry, Troy, I have to see someone in the morning before I drive back.'

'Then you'll just have to come to New York.'

When they got back to the table, Ryder was waiting for her. 'Forgive the interruption. Martha would like to see you before she goes home, Anna.'

'Right.' She collected her evening purse and smiled at Troy.

But when they crossed the now empty hall to the kitchen, Anna found that this was empty too, the caterers gone and no sign of Mrs Carter.

'What's all this about?' she demanded.

'I was concerned about you.' Ryder closed the door behind him and led her to a chair. 'Sit there for a moment and let me get you something to drink. You're beginning to look tired, Anna.'

She was beginning to feel tired too, but it was annoying to hear it from Ryder.

'Are you offering to make me hot chocolate?'

'I would if I had more time. Will some of Martha's stash of fizzy lemonade do?'

'Perfectly. Then I'll put some lipstick on and get back to the fray.'

'Eager to dance with Breckenridge again? Or do you prefer Toby?' he demanded, pouring lemonade into a glass.

'Neither for the moment.' She sipped thirstily. 'Actually, Squire, I'm going to join my father and the Jessops for a chat.'

'Good. I'll introduce you to the others at their table.' Ryder eyed her moodily as she got up and shook out her rustling skirts. 'You've lost weight.'

'Flattering dress,' she said dismissively and made for the small bathroom Mrs Carter used. 'You needn't wait for me.'

But when she emerged, lipstick bright, Ryder was ready like a warder waiting to take her back into custody. Anna walked back to the marquee with him in tense silence but, instead of taking her to her father, Ryder led her on to the dance floor.

'With all the others buzzing round you like bees round a honey pot I may not get another chance,' he said in her ear as he drew her close.

This time Ryder kept her on the floor for the entire set of three slow dances, holding her close in such complete silence that Anna was glad, at last, when a crash of cymbals brought the session to a close and he took her across the room to join her father and the Jessops and another couple at the table who were vaguely familiar to Anna from her childhood.

'I hardly recognised your sweet little tomboy, Dr Morton,' said Althea Knightley, smiling warmly. 'My sister was very fond of you, Anna.'

'She was always kind to me, Lady Knightley.' Anna smiled ruefully. 'Apparently I worried her a lot.'

'She just had to keep up with the boys,' said her father, patting her hand. 'My father had to watch her like a hawk to keep her in one piece.'

'Hector Morton was a fine man,' said Sir George. 'I did a lot of shooting here with him in the old days. I hear Ryder's going to hire someone to get the shoots going again, but your father's shoes will be hard to fill, Dr Morton.'

Anna spent several pleasant minutes in reminiscences, then turned to Helen to congratulate her on the flowers.

'My dear Mrs Jessop,' said Lady Knightley, impressed. 'Are these all your own work?'

Oliver Jessop smiled proudly. 'My wife is very artistic.'

'I had some help from ladies in my husband's congregation,' his wife pointed out honestly, and then smiled at Anna. 'On your feet again, dear. I see a determined young man approaching.'

The next hour went by in a blur of different partners as Anna danced with Toby Lonsdale, Dominic, Dick Hammond, Troy Breckenridge, and then, to her surprise, with his father. She had glimpses of Ryder with various partners, even at one point with Edwina French. But when the last dance was announced she saw Ryder make for her with such obvious intent that Troy retreated to the table to sit the last waltz out alone.

'Have you enjoyed this party better than the last one?' asked Ryder.

'I could hardly fail to. It was a fantastic evening, Ryder.'

'No comments about gamekeeper's brats tonight, then,' he said, holding her closer.

'No, indeed. In fact your uncle spoke about Gramp in glowing terms.'

'As most people do who knew him—except the local poachers. How soon are your father and Tom leaving tomorrow?'

'After breakfast, probably.'

'Ring me when they leave.'

As the band played a flourishing finale Ryder whirled Anna round with sudden panache and she clutched at him suddenly.

'What is it?' he demanded.

'Dizzy,' she said tersely. 'Too much champagne.'

'Or too much dancing,' he said grimly. 'I'd better get you back to your father so you can go straight home to bed.' He took her hand to walk off the floor, then looked round in surprise as Hartley Breckenridge took the stage to speak into the microphone.

He thanked Ryder at length for his hospitality, for this wonderful, memorable evening, and last but not least for giving the Breckenridge family the opportunity to meet the friends and family of young Dominic, who was soon to be the husband of his beloved daughter Hannah.

A roar of applause greeted the end of the speech as Hartley Breckenridge stepped off the stage to shake Ryder's hand and Anna slipped away to join her father.

'Can we get home now, Dad?' she begged. 'My feet are killing me.'

'So are mine. I was glad to sit this one out. Here's Tom,' he added as he saw his son approaching. 'We'll just say our goodbyes, then make our getaway.'

The following morning John Morton left straight after breakfast to make a full report to Nancy about the ball and Tom left soon afterwards.

'I'm taking Rachel out to lunch. What time are you leaving?' he asked, yawning, as Anna walked down the path with him.

'As soon as I can.' After Ryder had come to say what he had to say.

Anna waved him off, then went back into the house to shower and, as soon as her hair was dry and clasped in a sleek tail at the nape of her neck, she rang Ryder. 'My visitors have gone,' she reported.

'Right. I'm on my way.'

Anna made herself a cup of tea and took it to the window seat in the parlour to wait. Before the cup was empty, the Land Rover had parked behind her car and Ryder, in khaki sweater and cords, was striding up the path. She opened the door before he could knock and led him into the parlour.

'Good morning. You must be tired,' she said, feeling a sudden surge of panic now she was alone with him at last.

Ryder nodded. 'But the marquee won't be dismantled until tomorrow morning, thank God, so the house is peaceful for a while.'

'Is Mrs Carter in today?'

'No. She offered to stay once she'd served breakfast, but I sent her home after my relatives left. My American guests insist on taking me to lunch at the Over Court Hotel.' He eyed her quizzically. 'You know why I'm here, so why are we making small talk, Anna?'

'Let's sit down.' She took her usual seat on the sofa, but instead of joining her Ryder sat opposite and leaned forward, his eyes locked so purposefully on hers that Anna felt apprehensive.

'I might as well get straight to the point,' he began. 'I can't do this any more, Anna.'

Her heart did a nosedive. 'Do what?'

He held up his hands in surrender. 'To hell with my pride. I give in. We'll do it your way. I'll settle for whatever time we can snatch together.' He paused, eyeing her narrowly. 'But you don't want that any more, obviously.'

Anna's stomach gave a sickening lurch as she braced herself to answer. 'Ryder,' she said at last. 'When you asked me to stay here with you I had very specific reasons for turning you down.'

'I know.' Ryder sat back and folded his arms across his chest. 'You don't want children and you thought I'd cast you off when I found a potential bride who did.'

'Exactly.' She took in a deep breath and looked him in the eye. 'But fate plays some funny tricks. When I went down with pneumonia, it was the bacterial type that's treated with antibiotics and I hadn't finished the course when we met up again. Due to the antibiotics, the contraceptive pills I'd taken so faithfully didn't work.' Oh Lord, she thought in desperation, this was so hard. She took in a deep breath. 'I know you've heard this one before from Edwina, and the last thing you want is to hear it again from me, but I'm pregnant, Ryder.'

CHAPTER TWELVE

ANNA had gone through this scene in her mind countless times and the scenario had never gone as far as being swept into Ryder's arms with exclamations of delight. But she had expected a reaction of some kind from him. Instead he sat without moving a muscle, his eyes fixed on hers in complete silence.

'I know what you're going to say next,' she blurted at last.

'Do you?' he said conversationally.

'You're going to ask if the child really is yours.'

'Is it?'

Anna began to regret the toast she'd had for breakfast. 'This isn't a clever ploy to catch the wealthy heir instead of the younger brother, Ryder Wyndham. I hate the thought of being pregnant, but the child is most definitely yours.' She swallowed convulsively and then fled to the pantry to lean over the sink and lose what seemed like everything she'd eaten for days. A great time for morning sickness to start, she thought bitterly. She straightened warily, ran cold water into the sink, then splashed some on her face and buried it in a towel. When she looked up, Ryder was watching her in the kitchen doorway.

'Are you all right?' he asked

'No.' She looked at her watch. 'Time I was going.'

'Going?'

'Back to London.'

'You can't possibly drive in that state!'

'I can. And I will. Please let me pass.'

His eyes narrowed to hot blue slits. 'Not before we've settled this.'

Her chin lifted. 'There's nothing to settle. I've said my piece and, short though it was, you've most certainly said yours, so that's it. End of story.' She waited pointedly for him to move, but he stood barring her way.

'Are you going to keep the baby, Anna?' he asked, as though the words were wrenched from him.

She eyed him with disdain. 'No business of yours whether I do or not, Ryder.'

'If it's my child it is!'

'But you're in some doubt about that.' Anna gave him a disdainful smile. 'Just for the record, I hadn't been with another man since I broke up with Sean, over a year ago. Whether you believe it or not, you really are the father of my child. But don't worry. I don't aspire to anything as exalted as marriage between the Squire and the gamekeeper's brat. I just thought you had the right to know, and now you do. So get out of my house, please. I need to lock up.'

Ryder stood his ground, ignoring her. His mind raced as he tried to come to terms with the fact that Anna was expecting his child. Because he knew perfectly well that it was his. Anna was too much a product of her family's upbringing to lie to him. But the shock of her announcement had sent the old feeling of entrapment he'd felt with Edwina rushing through him and, for the second time in their lives, and with just two little words this time, he'd alienated Anna, probably for good. Which was unthinkable if she was soon to give birth to his heir. He felt as sick as Anna when he thought of Dr Morton's reaction, not to mention Tom's.

'Why didn't you tell me sooner?' he said at last.

Anna's eyes burned dark in her ashen face. 'I couldn't tell you something like that over the phone.' She looked away. 'Besides, at first I didn't realise what was wrong. I'd been ill and things were hectic at work—'

'Ah, yes, the job,' he said bitterly. 'Your first priority.'

'Top of my list at the moment,' she retorted, stung, 'is sorting out some maternity leave.'

'You can forget that.' Ryder closed the space between them and seized her hands. 'Your first priority now is to give in your notice and marry me, Anna, whether you want to or not. I won't have you endangering my child while you work all the hours God sends to prove you're as good as any man in your firm.'

'So it's *your* child now,' she said, incensed. 'It happens to be my child too, remember. I have no intention of endangering it.' Her eyes flashed. 'And I consider myself better than any man in my firm.'

'So do I. But let's forget the job for a moment.' Ryder looked at her searchingly. 'Have you seen a doctor?'

'Yes.' Anna felt her colour rise. 'But I'm not booked in anywhere yet because I wasn't sure what was going to happen.'

Ryder gave her a scornful look. 'You knew exactly what would happen once you told me, Anna.'

'I meant that I might go back to Shrewsbury, not come running to you to make an honest woman of me.' Her mouth twisted. 'But of course Wyndhams always do the right thing.'

'Just as my great-uncle Ned would have done if he'd been able to get back to Violet,' agreed Ryder. 'But he didn't get the chance. Since I do, I'll start putting things in motion right away. I suppose formal application to your father should be first on the list.'

'Not so fast.' Her eyes speared his. 'I haven't said I'll marry you, Ryder. You can contribute towards the child if you like, but I'll support myself.'

'My child will be brought up at Wyndham Manor,' he said flatly. 'Whether you make your home there too is up to you.' God, he thought in despair, what woman would accept an offer made in those terms?

Anna reacted in a way that put an abrupt end to the conversation. She turned away and began retching into the sink again, trying to push him away when he put his arm round her and held her head.

'Go away,' she gasped, when she could speak.

He wrung out the end of a towel in cold water and mopped her sweating forehead. 'Come and lie down, Anna. I'll make you some tea.'

'I don't want any tea,' she snapped, panting. 'I want you to go away and leave me alone.'

Ryder picked her up and carried her into the parlour. He carefully laid her on a sofa and stood back. 'Do you use your car much in London?' he asked her.

She stared at him blankly. 'No, I go to work by bus. Why?'

'If you really must get back to London today, I'll drive you to Hereford to catch a train, then you return the same way next weekend and I'll pick you up from the station.'

Anna thought it over. Right now the thought of driving anywhere made her stomach heave. The sensible move was to stay put at the cottage and travel back in the morning. Even take the whole day off. She would ring the office and plead a stomach bug. Which wasn't so far out. 'No need for that, Ryder,' she said at last. 'I'll stay here today and drive back tomorrow. Now go, please. Your guests are waiting.'

'I'll come back after lunch to check on you.'

'I'd rather you didn't.'

His eyes hardened. 'Quite possibly, but I will anyway.'

Once she heard Ryder drive away, Anna got very slowly to her feet, then went to make the tea she'd refused from Ryder. She took it back to the sofa, drank every drop of it, then stretched out, deep in miserable thought for a long time before she fell into a heavy dreamless sleep. She woke to hammering on the door and got up, yawning, to open it.

'Where the hell were you?' Ryder demanded. He eyed her pallid face closely. 'How do you feel?'

Anna pushed at strands of escaping hair as she closed the door. 'Better,' she said at last. 'Didn't you go out to lunch?'

'I went, I ate, and then drove back to check on you,' he said tersely.

She stared at her watch in shock. 'Good heavens, is that time?' She pulled at her sweater in distaste. 'I must change.'

'After that we talk. And you should have something to eat.'

She opened her mouth to refuse, then changed her mind. Why shouldn't he wait on her? 'Some toast would be good.'

Anna went upstairs very slowly and gave an accusing look at her bed. If she hadn't let Ryder make love to her there, she wouldn't be in her present situation. But she had and Lord knew it had been a wonderful experience, so if she had to get pregnant at least her baby was the result of joy rather than the routine it had dwindled to with Sean.

When she went downstairs Ryder had a tray of tea and toast waiting in the parlour.

'Sit down, Anna,' he ordered. 'You know that there's only one solution to all this. Will you marry me?'

She nibbled on a piece of toast, then drank some tea before giving her answer. 'I've had time to think since you left, so, in spite of our mutual regret about the motive for your proposal, the answer's yes.' She shrugged. 'But let's be clear about this, Ryder. I'm not doing it for my sake, not just for the child's, but because I couldn't bear to spoil things for my father just when he's so happy about getting married again. Tom wouldn't be very thrilled, either. Not,' she added quickly as Ryder winced, 'that he'd mind in the least about having a single parent for a sister, but—'

'He'd find it hard to forgive me for being responsible,' said Ryder bitterly, 'your father too.'

'Yes. They both think the world of you. This way they'll be surprised, but they'll keep their illusions.' Anna gave him a hostile look. 'Unfortunately, to achieve that, the Wyndham heir will be saddled with a socially inferior bride.'

'For God's sake stop thinking of yourself that way!' he said explosively.

'Oh, I don't, Ryder. But you do. Your gut reaction to me as Dominic's wife confirmed that.' She smiled in mock pity. 'Heaven knows how you must be feeling now I'm going to be yours.'

'Let's leave my feelings out of it.' His eyes blazed for an instant, then dulled. 'So now we've got all that out of the way, we'd better get married as soon as possible. I'll have a word with the vicar tomorrow—'

'No,' she said flatly.

'I must, Anna, if we're to get a wedding arranged here at such short notice,' he said impatiently.

'Hannah's getting married in New York.'

Ryder looked at her narrowly. 'And your point is?'

'Her parents turned down a wedding here in favour of their own home, Ryder. My father will too, when he knows.'

'I see.' He shrugged. 'Very well, what do you want, then, Anna?'

'I *want* not to be pregnant, with no wedding necessary,' she snapped. 'But, since I am, and it is, I suggest a register office ceremony in Shrewsbury and a small reception afterwards in my own home.'

'Whatever you say, Anna. Something warns me not to kiss you, so shall we shake hands to seal the bargain?'

Since for the moment Anna couldn't cope with the thought of any contact with him, however slight, she ignored him and finished her tea.

'Talking of hands,' said Ryder after a moment's silence, 'I must provide you with a ring.'

'A plain gold band is the only one necessary,' she said firmly. 'Unlike Edwina French, I don't require diamonds.'

'Possibly not, but I think your father and Tom would find it strange if I didn't give you an engagement ring of some kind.' Ryder leaned forward. 'Look, Anna, I know this isn't what you want—'

'It's not what you want, either!'

'It has its plus side,' he assured her. 'I'm getting a chartered accountant for a wife and a child into the bargain, so things could be a lot worse.'

'You expect me to work for you?' she demanded.

'Not if you object. But, knowing you, Anna, I thought you'd want to.'

He was right, she thought mutinously.

'What I'm trying to get across,' he went on, 'is that we should make the best of things. We already know each other better than most couples ever do. Added to that, we're highly compatible in bed—'

'You expect that side of our relationship to carry on?' she said, frowning.

'I most certainly do.' His eyes locked with hers. 'Let's get that straight from the start. You may be an unwilling bride, Anna, but make no mistake. I intend our marriage to be normal in every way.'

'I see.'

Ryder got up and went to the window to stare out at the tidy garden. 'Where would you like to go for a honeymoon?'

Anna stared in surprise at his rigid back. 'Honeymoon?'

'It's the usual procedure.'

'I don't want to go anywhere. I'd rather stay at home.'

Ryder turned sharply. 'Home?'

Time for an olive branch, decided Anna. 'With the Manor and the entire Wyndham Estate at our disposal, why travel elsewhere?'

'You're ready to start thinking of the Manor as home, then?' he said, relieved.

She smiled wryly. 'Resigned rather than ready. It's hard to see myself fitting into your life, Ryder.'

'I can't see why. You had no problem with that last night,' he reminded her.

'That was as your guest. Living there as your wife is another story.'

He crossed the room and, to her surprise, lifted her hand to his lips and kissed it. 'I'll do everything in my power to make sure the story has a happy ending, Anna. You have my word.'

A maximum of six weeks proved to be necessary to organise the wedding, for which Anna was grateful. It gave her time to give a month's notice to her employers, and for Dominic and Hannah to arrange another trip to the UK. Both of them were delighted with the news, though Dominic told his brother it was no surprise.

'You two were always meant for each other. No one who came to the ball will be surprised—including Hannah. She told me you were both head over heels about each other, old friends or not.'

Anna was quite glad of the time to sort out the changes in her life. Clare was an unfailing support and offered to spend the intervening weekends with Charlie so Ryder could stay at the flat, but Anna refused.

'We'll have plenty of time together after we're married,' she said firmly.

'But surely you're going to see Ryder before the wedding?' said Clare, astonished.

'Yes. Dad's invited him to Shrewsbury next weekend to meet Nancy. She's cooking a celebration lunch and Tom's bringing Rachel to meet us. But I'm not driving down,' said Anna with a yawn and patted her flat midriff. 'We're going by train.'

Anna arrived in Shrewsbury early on the Saturday and, after an emotional talk with her father, took his advice and spent the afternoon in bed to prepare herself for Ryder's arrival in the evening.

When she saw his car turn into the drive, Anna felt so tense with nerves as she watched him reach in the car for his suit jacket she was trembling by the time she opened the door to him.

'Hello,' she said brightly. 'Good journey?'

Looking his spectacular best in a magnificent suit and a shirt which matched his eyes, Ryder took her by the shoulders and kissed her cheek gently. 'Never mind the small talk, tell me how you are. You look tired.'

'She shouldn't be,' said John Morton, running down the stairs. 'She slept all afternoon. Don't worry, Ryder, I'm taking good care of her.'

Ryder kept an arm round Anna as he shook hands with her father. 'I promise that I'll take good care of her too,' he said gravely.

After the simple cold supper John Morton served them he excused himself to offer help to Nancy for the celebration meal the next day.

When they were alone Anna took Ryder into the conservatory to watch the sun set over the long, narrow garden at the back of the house.

'Your father was obviously being tactful about giving us time together,' said Ryder as they sat together on a wicker sofa.

'Or he just wants to spend time with Nancy.'

'I've got something for you, Anna.' Ryder took a twist of tissue paper from his pocket. 'You can't be engaged properly without a ring. I could have bought you a rock like Dominic gave Hannah, but I thought you might prefer this.'

Anna's eyes widened as she unwrapped a heavy gold ring. It was obviously old by the setting, with two diamonds flanking a central stone the colour of Ryder's eyes. 'How perfectly lovely!'

'It's really a dress ring my mother wore on her right hand as something old and blue on her wedding day.' He slid it on her finger. 'Good. It's only a fraction too loose.'

'I love the blue stone,' she said, admiring it. 'What is it?'

'The jeweller who cleaned it up for you says it's a Brazilian aquamarine of unusual depth of colour.'

'Thank you, Ryder.' She smiled at him. 'I'm glad you didn't get a rock. I'd much rather have something that belonged to your mother.'

He put a finger under her chin. 'Do I get a kiss by way of thanks?'

Anna looked up at him steadily. 'Do you want one?'

Instead of answering, Ryder bent his head and kissed her long and hard. 'Since you ask, yes,' he said gruffly. 'In fact, I want a whole lot more than that. But I can wait.'

On the day she left her job, Anna returned to the flat laden with presents from her colleagues at the firm. 'There,' she said to

Clare, as her friend relieved her of her parcels. 'I've burnt my boats. I'm unemployed.'

Clare touched her midriff. 'How do you feel?'

'Fat.'

'Rubbish. You've just made up some of the weight you lost in the beginning.'

'What if I don't fit into my dress by next week?'

'After the search we had to find one you liked, I jolly well hope so. It's a size bigger than usual, remember, and that clever draping in front will hide any tendency to bulge—which you don't.'

'Yet,' said Anna grimly, and sighed. 'My brown jersey silk drapes too. I could have worn that and saved myself a lot of money and hassle.'

'Your father would have a fit if you'd turned up for your wedding in something you'd had for years!'

'Which was my sole reason for buying something new. I just hope I can still fit into it when it's time for *his* wedding.' Anna grinned. 'We just need Tom to marry Rachel and we'll have a full set.'

'Is that likely?'

'After seeing them together at the lunch that weekend, I think it's highly likely. He's bringing her to the wedding, so you can see for yourself.'

Anna went home to Shrewsbury for the few remaining days before the wedding to spend time with her father. She saw a lot of Nancy and Grace, and her godson was such a charmer that Anna began to feel it might not be so bad to be a mother after all. Her only contact with Ryder was by telephone in bed at night when he brought her up to date with estate news and the progress of Hood and Hardy, the puppies he'd named after two captains in Lord Nelson's band of brothers.

'Dick and Jen have done a great job on them, but they're going back to the farm until after the wedding so Martha can decorate the cake in peace,' said Ryder. 'Hannah and Dominic fly in on Thursday and they're bringing Martha to Shrewsbury, leaving me to transport the cake.'

'I hope the cake wasn't too much work for Mrs Carter.'

'She's in her element. Carol and Alison have taken over the lion's share of the cleaning to leave Martha free to wield her icing gun. I can't tell you what it's like because I'm not allowed to see it until it's finished. Now, tell me how you are.'

'Dr Morton is satisfied his daughter's in rude health.'

'That's good. Are you reconciled to the idea of a baby yet?'

'I'm getting there.' She took in a deep breath. 'I just hope I can do it, Ryder.'

'Do what?'

'Cope with motherhood half as well as Grace does. She makes it look so easy.'

'I doubt that it is. Though I'm sure you will cope. You were changing Dominic's nappies when you were only ten, remember. But don't think about that for now, Anna. You're going to be a bride before you're a mother. In four days' time, remember.'

'As if I could forget!'

Other than a slight episode of nausea when she first woke up, Anna enjoyed her wedding day far more than she'd expected. The sun shone, her bulge was undetectable under the clever draping of her ivory silk dress and the subtle almond-pink of her extravagant straw hat lent a glow of colour to her face. Ryder was waiting for her outside the register office, with Toby Lonsdale in support, so breathtakingly handsome in his formal morning clothes that she faltered for a moment. Then her father kissed her lovingly as he handed her over to Ryder and the four of them went inside to join the friends and relatives gathered to witness the marriage of Anna Frances Morton and Ryder Francis Wyndham.

Anna was tired by the time Ryder turned down the drive to the Manor later that night. The wedding reception had been lively and because the weather had been kind the caterers were able to serve the meal in the garden. The speeches were mercifully short—Dr Morton's a little sentimental, Ryder's polished and graceful, but Toby Lonsdale's caused much laughter when he praised the beauty of the bride.

'When I met her at the dance recently I didn't recognise her. In the past she was invariably soaking wet or caked with mud,' he said, grinning at Anna. 'I had no idea she scrubbed up so well.'

'Martha's left a cold supper for us, but I've given her the week off,' said Ryder as they reached Little Over. 'I thought you might prefer to settle in on your own for a few days.'

'Good idea. Is she going away?'

'Her friend, George Latham, is treating her to a week in the Lake District, apparently.'

Anna felt touched when Ryder drove through the gatehouse to park the car at the foot of the portico steps at the grand front entrance. She followed him up to the big double doors, finding it hard to believe this was all real as he unlocked them. Expecting him to stand aside to allow her in first, she gave a squeak of surprise when Ryder picked her up and carried her inside the lofty hall, clicking on switches as he went to illuminate the exquisite arrangement of flowers in the great urn at the foot of the stairs.

'Welcome home, Mrs Wyndham,' he said huskily as he set her on her feet.

'Thank you, Mr Wyndham,' she said, smiling at him. 'Mrs Jessop got to work before she came to the wedding, obviously.'

'It seemed like a good idea to ask her. She's put flowers in the morning room too. I'll get the luggage in. Do you want to unpack before supper?'

'Just the smallest bag,' she said, feeling ridiculously shy. 'I'll do the rest tomorrow.'

When Ryder came back with the suitcases, he told her to follow him upstairs. 'Come with me so you'll know where I've put everything.'

When he put all her belongings in his bedroom Anna knew that Ryder was making it clear that he intended her to share it with him.

'I'll help you unpack tomorrow,' he said, as he put her overnight bag on the ottoman at the foot of his bed. 'Come down when you're ready. I'll be in the morning room.'

Anna spent some time in Ryder's bathroom—her bathroom too now, she reminded herself. She touched up her face, released her hair from the sleek coil she'd worn under her hat, then eyed her full length reflection critically. Her new white cotton jersey trousers had elastic in the waistband and the pink voile shirt she wore loose over them had plenty of room to spare to accommodate the heir to Wyndham Manor. But, other than a new opulence in the curves under her shirt, she looked much the same as usual.

When she joined Ryder in the morning room, their supper was waiting on the table, with candles in silver holders and champagne waiting in a bucket of ice. Anna smiled wryly at Ryder as he held out her chair.

'This looks very romantic.'

'Since I worked so hard to achieve the effect, I'm glad you think so.' His eyes smiled with such significance into hers that she felt her throat thicken. 'I promise to try my best to make you happy, Anna.'

She shook her head. 'No trying necessary, Ryder. Now we've tied the knot it's up to both of us to make our marriage work.'

'The fact remains that I said the wrong thing when you gave me the news. Do you think you can ever forgive me?' he asked.

'I'm working on it,' she said honestly. 'But right now let's eat. I'm hungry.'

Ryder poured champagne, then raised his glass in a toast. 'To the three of us.'

Anna smiled, touched, as she lifted her glass to his. 'To the three of us.'

They talked over the wedding as they ate the simple salad meal Martha had left for them. But afterwards Anna smiled in delight when Ryder put a perfect small replica of the wedding cake in front of her.

'It's too perfect to cut. How sweet of Mrs Carter.'

'She thinks the world of you,' Ryder informed her and smiled, his eyes gleaming like sapphires in the candlelight. 'She told me I'd made the right choice this time.'

'That's nice. I'm surprised she approves, though,' said Anna, draining her glass.

'Are you referring to our social differences again?' said Ryder with menace. 'Because if you are, baby or no baby, I'll get violent.'

'Promises, promises,' mocked Anna recklessly.

Ryder stood up and walked round the table to help her up. 'Come on, Mrs Wyndham, time you were in bed.'

'Are you coming to bed too?'

'A strange question for a bride to ask on her wedding night,' he said wryly. 'Of course I am. We're going to leave all this until tomorrow and go to bed right now. Together.'

As they walked up stairs which felt a little unsteady beneath Anna's feet, she smiled cheerfully at the portraits as they passed. She was a Wyndham now too, whether they liked it or not.

'Your family now,' said Ryder, reading her mind, then caught her hand as she stumbled on the top step. 'Come on,' he said, picking her up. 'I think that second glass of champagne was a mistake.'

'It was Dutch courage, not champagne,' she admitted. 'I'm nervous.'

He grinned, looking so much more like the Ryder of old that she relaxed against him. 'Honest to the last, Anna.'

When they reached his room Ryder set her on her feet, then pulled her close, his lips on hers in a kiss of such sudden, open demand that it lit up erogenous zones Anna found she still possessed in abundance, pregnant or not. He sat down on the bed and drew her on to his lap, kissing and caressing her until they were both breathless and shaken. At last he tore his mouth away and leaned his forehead against hers. 'Are you still nervous? I hope not, because I want you badly, Anna. For God's sake say you want me.'

For answer she slid off his lap and held out her arms, her eyes luminous with invitation and in minutes they were naked in each other's arms in his bed, tears on Anna's cheeks at they held each other close. 'I've missed you so *much*, Ryder.'

'I'm deliriously happy to hear it, but please don't cry, darling.'

'My hormones are crying, not me.'

He chuckled and licked away her tears, trying to control the passion lying in wait. 'God, how I've hungered for the taste of you. I've lain awake in this bed, night after night after you left, cursing myself for making love to you here.'

Anna threaded her fingers through his glossy, tumbled hair as she rubbed her cheek against his. 'I haven't slept well either. It wasn't the sex I missed so much—'

'Lucky you,' he said dryly and laughed when she dug indignant fingers into his back.

'I missed the closeness and the sense of belonging,' she said huskily.

Ryder propped himself on an elbow to look down into her face. 'I still can't believe my luck in making you pregnant, but if I hadn't would you have come back to me?'

'Oh, yes.' Anna smiled at him ruefully. 'In the end I couldn't have stayed away. I found out for sure that I was pregnant just after I received your invitation to the ball. I decided to buy the most fabulous dress I could find and dazzle you so much you'd fall on one knee and propose next day when I told you I was expecting your baby. Unfortunately, it didn't work out quite like that.'

He buried his face in her hair in remorse. 'I'll spend the rest of my life trying to make that up to you. But here we are, husband and wife, and I think the time has come to make my confession.'

'No,' she said in alarm. 'I don't want to hear it.'

'Sorry. I insist.' He raised his head, the look in his eyes taking her breath away. 'I love you, Anna. I always have in one way or another, right back since you were eight years old. Do you love me?'

'Of course I do,' she said crossly. 'Why else do you think I married you?'

Ryder gave a shout of laughter, then kissed her hard, the kiss quickly turning into something so hot and electric they came together in a frenzy of seeking hands and mouths, and bodies that fused together in mounting, heart-stopping rapture that left them shaken and dazed in each other's arms afterwards as their hearts slowed.

'I hope,' said Ryder at last, 'that our first-born coped with that.'

Anna's head flew up. 'First-born? You want me to do this more than once?'

He shuddered and held her close. 'Hell, no, darling, I don't. I hate the thought of putting you through it this time. I'll only breathe easy once he arrives safely and I know all is well with you.'

'Ryder,' said Anna gently. 'You do realise it might be a she, not a he.'

'In which case,' he said with emphasis, 'that's it, game over. Dominic can provide the heirs.'

In the middle of a cold night the following December Anna woke her husband by shaking him mercilessly. He shot upright, protesting, then saw her face and leapt out of bed.

'My waters broke,' she said tersely and watched in amazement as in a split second her expensively educated husband changed into a gibbering maniac.

'Oh, God—I'll get the car,' he said, racing towards the door, then stopped dead and ran back to her. 'Are you all right, darling?'

'Not—really—' she said through gritted teeth.

'Where's your suitcase?' he asked wildly.

'Where it's been for a month—in the car.'

'I should ring the hospital—'

'I've already done that. Get *dressed*, Ryder.'

'Yes. Right.' He started pulling on the clothes he'd left on a chair ready for precisely this emergency, clumsy in his haste. 'You'd better get dressed too, darling.'

'I am dressed, Ryder—' She broke off to pant. 'Could we just go, please?'

He seized her hand and led her from the room. 'Careful, sweetheart,' he said anxiously as they negotiated the curve of the stairs, his heart pounding when Anna had to lean on the banisters halfway down as another pain stopped her in her tracks. Ryder looked on helplessly while she panted, his eyes frantic in his white face. 'Shall I carry you down?'

'And give you a slipped disc?' she said breathlessly. 'I'm a bit heavier than the day you carried me over the threshold, remember. I'd rather you just held my hand again while I make it on my own two feet, darling.'

Ryder kissed her fiercely, then walked with her step by step down the rest of the staircase and across the hall, leaving her leaning against a pillar in the hall while he ran outside to start the car.

By noon next day Ryder Wyndham was such a hindrance in the labour ward the midwife told him to get some coffee and take a break while his wife got on with the job in hand.

'Good idea,' Anna panted gratefully.

'Are you sure?' demanded Ryder.

'Yes!'

He bent to kiss her perspiring forehead. 'I won't be long.' He gave her a last anguished glance as he went out.

'Right,' said the midwife briskly. 'Now Daddy's out of the way, let's get on with it, shall we? A few good pushes and we'll be there, Mrs Wyndham.'

Anna gave vent to the kind of visceral groan she'd fought to control while Ryder was on hand and pushed with all her might. A few minutes later her son was born, protesting loudly as he slithered into the hands of a waiting nurse.

'Is he all right?' gasped Anna.

'Perfect in every detail,' said the midwife and wiped the perspiration from Anna's forehead. 'You can see for yourself soon—but no peace for the wicked, it's time to push again.'

When Ryder was let into the room later, his wife was propped against pillows holding a small bundle in each arm. He bent to kiss her weary, smiling face, unashamed tears on the lashes fringing the famous Wyndham eyes. 'How do you feel, my darling?'

'Tired. No wonder they call it labour—having babies is very hard work!'

He grinned and kissed her again. 'Not from my point of view.' He looked down in wonder at the tiny identical faces, then tensed in panic as the midwife took the babies from Anna and handed them to him one at a time.

'Have a little cuddle before I take them off to get sorted. Then I suggest you go home and have a rest, Mr Wyndham, and come back when your wife has had a nice sleep.'

When they were alone Ryder drew Anna very gently into his arms. 'Are you really all right?'

'Yes, but I'm glad it's over,' she admitted, 'and now I know the twins came with a complete set of everything I would quite like a sleep.' She smiled suddenly, her dark eyes sparkling up at him above the smudges of fatigue. 'You get some sleep, too, Daddy, while you can. We won't get much once we take the twins home.'

A few weeks later Ryder Wyndham sat up in bed, watching his wife brush her hair at the dressing table. 'I never tire of watching you do that, Anna.'

'Since the twins were born I've had serious thoughts about having it cut off to make life easier. On the other hand, it's very low maintenance this way. Short hair needs cutting regularly and at the moment I can't spare the time.' She turned to smile at him. 'In mediaeval times when women's hair was hidden, taking it down in the privacy of the marriage chamber told her lord and master she was in a receptive mood.'

Ryder shot out of bed and crossed the room to pick her up. 'In that case, stop brushing and come to bed.'

Anna laughed and kissed him as he carried her across the room, then gave a sigh of pleasure as they stretched out together under the covers. 'It went well in church today, didn't it? The twins yelled when the vicar splashed them with water, which sent their godparents into a panic, but otherwise they behaved better than I expected.'

'I'm more interested in whether they behave themselves tonight.' He kissed her. 'I love my children, but after the long months of celibacy I would deeply appreciate half an hour's peace to make love to their mother now it's possible at last.'

'Mmm, me too,' she sighed and grinned at him. 'Only half an hour? After all this time I was hoping for longer than that.'

Ryder laughed as he began kissing her, but the laughter was soon over as his caresses grew urgent, Anna's eyes brilliant with love as she arched her body to take him deep inside her. Ryder gave a deep, relishing groan of pleasure and rained kisses all over her face as they began to scale the heights of rapture, the rhythm of their loving accelerating until they reached the ultimate peak together.

'It's so quiet. Have I died and gone to heaven?' whispered Ryder as they lay together afterwards in sated languor.

Anna stretched luxuriously against him. 'Maybe you turned the baby mike off.'

Ryder stretched out an arm to investigate, then laughed softly as he heard unmistakable sounds of heavy breathing through the monitor. 'No—still asleep. We might manage a few more moments' peace yet.'

'Oh, yes, please. I love my children, but we deserve some time together.' Anna turned her face up to his. 'This has been such an eventful year, Ryder. Not only with four weddings and a funeral, but a christening too.'

'It was touching to see your father today with the twins. And he's obviously very happy with Nancy.'

'As well he might be. She's a darling, my stepmother. But

Tom's lady is a live wire. With Rachel in his life my big brother is unlikely to be bored any time soon.'

'Boredom won't be a problem for me, either—the twins will see to that! You know, darling, it's incredible to think that it's only just over a year since I saw you at Hector's funeral,' said Ryder, holding her closer. 'I took one look that day and decided I had to make you forgive me somehow.'

'You succeeded. It didn't take you long to persuade me into bed!'

'Or to get you pregnant—with twins, at that.'

'Boaster,' she protested, giving him a shove.

'A man has every right to be in such ego-boosting circumstances.' Ryder planted a kiss on her mouth. 'And for someone who disliked motherhood in theory, you're so good at it in practice you've got plenty to boast about yourself, Anna Wyndham.'

'After producing Francis and Hector, I most certainly do.' She smiled up at him triumphantly. 'After all, I'm one up on previous Wyndham brides, Ryder. Reluctant mother I may have been to start with, but in the end I provided you with an heir and a spare at my very first attempt!'

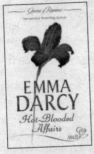

4 FREE

BOOKS AND A SURPRISE GIFT!

We would like to take this opportunity to thank you for reading this Mills & Boon® book by offering you the chance to take FOUR more specially selected titles from the Modern Romance™ series absolutely FREE! We're also making this offer to introduce you to the benefits of the Mills & Boon® Reader Service™—

- ★ **FREE home delivery**
- ★ **FREE gifts and competitions**
- ★ **FREE monthly Newsletter**
- ★ **Exclusive Reader Service offers**
- ★ **Books available before they're in the shops**

Accepting these FREE books and gift places you under no obligation to buy, you may cancel at any time, even after receiving your free shipment. Simply complete your details below and return the entire page to the address below. You don't even need a stamp!

YES! Please send me 4 free Modern Romance books and a surprise gift. I understand that unless you hear from me, I will receive 6 superb new titles every month for just £2.89 each, postage and packing free. I am under no obligation to purchase any books and may cancel my subscription at any time. The free books and gift will be mine to keep in any case.

P7ZED

Ms/Mrs/Miss/Mr ....Initials ....

BLOCK CAPITALS PLEASE

Surname ....

Address ....

....

....Postcode..................................

Send this whole page to:
UK: FREEPOST CN81, Croydon, CR9 3WZ